LILLIPUT

LILLIPUT

Sam Gayton

Illustrated by Alice Ratterree

PEACHTREE
ATLANTA

Published by
PEACHTREE PUBLISHERS
1700 Chattahoochee Avenue
Atlanta, Georgia 30318-2112
www.peachtree-online.com

Text © 2013 by Sam Gayton
Illustrations © 2015 by Alice Ratterree

First published in Great Britain in 2013 by Andersen Press Limited
First United States version published in 2015 by Peachtree Publishers
First United States trade paperback edition published in 2017

Design and composition by Nicola Simmonds Carmack

Illustrations rendered in pencil and watercolor

Printed in July 2017 by Lake Book Manufacturing in Melrose Park, Illinois, in the United States of America
10 9 8 7 6 5 4 3 2 1 (hardcover)
10 9 8 7 6 5 4 3 2 1 (trade paperback)

Library of Congress Cataloging-in-Publication Data

Gayton, Sam, author.
  Lilliput / by Sam Gayton ; illustrated by Alice Ratterree.
    pages cm
  ISBN 978-1-56145-806-6 (hardcover) / 978-1-68263-006-8 (trade paperback)
  Summary: Three-inch-tall Lily has been trapped in a bird cage for half of her life while her giant captor, Gulliver, writes a book about his travels but she finally escapes and, aided by a clockmaker's apprentice and his friends, makes plans to leave London and return home to Lilliput. Inspired by Jonathan Swift's novel, *Gulliver's Travels*.
  [1. Rescues—Fiction. 2. Size—Fiction. 3. Apprentices—Fiction. 4. Gulliver, Lemuel (Fictitious character)—Fiction. 5. Characters in literature—Fiction. 6. Fantasy. 7. London (England)—History—18th century—Fiction. 8. Great Britain—History—George II, 1727-1760—Fiction.] I. Ratterree, Alice, illustrator. II. Swift, Jonathan, 1667-1745. Gulliver's travels. III. Title.
  PZ7.G2416Lil 2015
  [E]—dc23
                                        2015002405

To Mum,
who is also Boss

—S. G.

CONTENTS

Prologue: CATCHING

Part One: ESCAPING

Part Two: SEARCHING

Part Three: LEAVING

Epilogue: RETURNING

Afterword

Prologue
CATCHING

To the Giants' Country
he lost his way;
They kept him there
for a year and a day.

—William Brighty Rands,
"Stalky Jack"

Pinchers & Plips

All down the pebble path to the beach, Lily sulked about her iron shoes. They clang-clang-clanged on her feet as she made her way to the shore. It was blowy and the waves were high as houses. Bellin was already there with his grumpy older sister Bree. They dug through the sucking wet sand, looking for pincher crabs.

Lily stomped toward them, iron shoes flashing in the sun. Bree scowled and nudged her brother, and Bellin pulled his tweezers from the beach and threw them with a plonk into his bucket. Together they watched her coming down the dunes to the wet sand left by the tide.

"Can I dig with you?" Lily asked, looking at Bellin.

"Suppose so," Bree muttered, rolling her eyes. She pointed down at Lily's shoes. "But take those off first."

Lily hesitated. A part of her wanted to, but the shoes were bound to her feet by more than just leather straps. "I can't," she said at last.

"You have to," said Bree. "All your stomping will

scare off the pinchers. Me and Bellin leave ours over there." She pointed at two pairs of rusty iron shoes over by the dunes. "Come on, Lily. Don't be a little'un."

Lily sniffed and shook her head again. "Can't," she repeated.

"You can," Bree insisted. "It's not dangerous, as long as you're careful."

Lily flung down her bucket and sat on a cockleshell, glaring at her feet. "That's what I said to Nana. But she never listens. She makes me promise."

Bree threw up her hands in frustration and looked over to her brother, but Bellin just shrugged. He grabbed his giant tweezers again and went back to rummaging.

They all knew why Lily's nana had made her promise. Catching pinchers was dangerous. The crabs dug themselves into the sucking sand, and if any hands or feet sank down close to them, they would snip off a finger or toe with their claws.

That was why they used giant tweezers to pull up pincher crabs, and wore iron shoes. But iron shoes were heavy and the pinchers always hid when they heard them.

Bree was older than Lily, and Bellin was braver. They always took their shoes off, so they could tiptoe up above the pinchers and take them by surprise.

But Lily never did. Nana made her promise every

time she went out crabbing, and though she sulked, she was also secretly glad. Lily liked her toes and she wanted to keep them.

Picking up her own tweezers, she climbed from the cockleshell, looking for a good spot of sand to rummage in.

"You're still a little'un." Bree folded her arms. "You shouldn't be here."

Lily felt herself go hot with embarrassment. "I'm six moons old," she told Bree angrily. "*You're* only seven."

"But I know how to catch pinchers."

"Then why is your bucket empty?"

"Come share my spot, Lily," said Bellin, stepping in front of his sister. "There's lots of space by me."

Bree hissed in anger and tugged her bucket farther away to another patch of sand.

"Don't listen to her," Bellin said quietly. "She thinks you're scaring the pinchers away, but you're not. They were dug down deep before you even got here."

Lily smiled. Her lips were dry and she licked them wet again. She scanned the beach. It was a hot spring day. Just a few squiggles of cloud and all the rest blue. Strange. Usually when it was warm the pincher crabs came up almost to the surface to sunbathe. But not today. Today, they were all hiding.

"Something has them scared," she told Bellin.

4

He shrugged and wiped the sweat from his brow. "Maybe it's Bree's temper," he whispered.

Lily's giggle became a gasp. Bellin tugged at something, then stood up straight, a huge pincher wriggling and clacking in his tweezers. It was as big as a dinner plate.

"Here's a brave one. It's not hiding like the rest." Bellin dropped it with a rattle into Lily's bucket. "Have it. Take it back to your nana. Everyone in Plips knows she makes the best pincher-crab pie in the village."

Lily grinned. "I will. And I'll tell her to save you the biggest slice. Thanks, Bellin."

Bellin shrugged.

Behind him his sister screamed.

At first Lily thought that Bree had been snipped by a pincher's claw. But she hadn't. She was pointing at the sea. Her body was rigid, and her tweezers lay forgotten in the sand.

Lily and Bellin turned, following her finger to where the waves were galloping back and forth over the shore. They both saw the head rise up from the spray, and the arms. Then the legs, wading out of the water.

He was so enormous Lily couldn't believe it. But there he was. Climbing out of all the stories Nana told her at bedtime.

A giant.

A mountain of a man.

He stood there, sea dripping from his hair, waves roaring at his feet. From the pockets of his coat he took an enormous pair of spectacles, the size and shape of a bicycle, and balanced them on his nose. His head moved left, then right.

And he saw them.

Suddenly Bellin's hand fell into Lily's and it was pulling her, dragging her back up the beach. They left the buckets and tweezers and fled for the dunes.

Lily couldn't keep up. The iron shoes were too heavy and she couldn't stop to untie them. Bellin's hand slipped from hers. Bree was on the shingle path, screaming for them to hurry.

Bellin caught up with his sister, and he turned to shout for Lily, but Bree dragged him off into the dunes. Behind them Lily tripped, fell, rose, and stumbled. She felt the rumbling steps of the giant, coming closer.

Closer, closer, closer, with his hands stretching out.

At last Lily reached the dunes and crawled into a hiding place in the grass. Gasping, she lay down and listened. The waves crashed and the wind blew and each breath rasped in her throat and that was all.

Make him go, she kept praying to the Ender. *Make him turn back to the sea.*

Then everything went darker, but the clouds had all unraveled from the sky.

Lily was sitting in his shadow. It was huge. It stretched out in front of her. Somewhere ahead, Bellin and Bree were screaming.

"Run, Lily! Run, run, run!"

She didn't even take a step. The giant was too quick. He scooped her into his palm, rough and lined. It bore her up like a flying carpet, and the beach fell away from the sky, and Bellin and Bree's voices fell away from her ears, and the sand trickled away through the giant's hand.

"Fair tidings to you, child of Lilliput!"

Lily opened her eyes. The giant was speaking. His voice boomed in her ears.

"If my speech sounds strange to your ears, apologies. I learned to speak Lilliputian over two hundred moons ago, in the court of Emperor Mully Ully Gue the First. No doubt the language since then has altered considerably. Indeed, I imagine almost everything in Lilliput has changed since last I was here. The emperor's great-great-great-grandson must sit on the throne now, yes?"

Lily gazed up, dumb with terror. The enormous face hung in the sky like a new moon, with its sloping cheeks, its cragged mountain of a nose, and the thousand little craters that pockmarked his skin.

"My name is Lemuel Gulliver," the giant continued in Lilliputian. "I should like to explain more to you, but we must leave at once. A great journey looms ahead of us, and the sooner we set sail for England, the sooner we shall arrive."

His spectacles flashed in the sun. Lily blinked and started, at last, to scream. Gulliver waited some time for her to stop. She did not. She screamed and screamed, then drew in another great gasp and screamed again, until the giant's palm tipped and Lily fell down into darkness.

Gulliver patted his pocket closed. Then he turned on his heel and began to walk. Back over the dunes, across the beach, and into the sea.

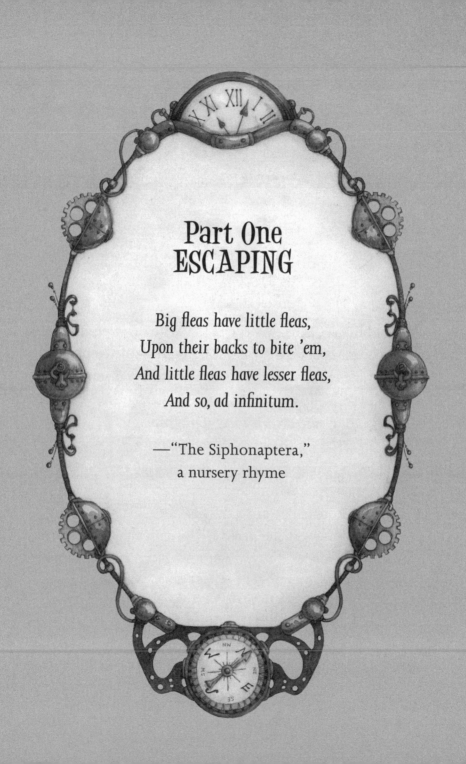

Part One
ESCAPING

Big fleas have little fleas,
Upon their backs to bite 'em,
And little fleas have lesser fleas,
And so, ad infinitum.

—"The Siphonaptera,"
a nursery rhyme

1

Scuttle & the Birdcage

The birdcage had tall, elegant sides with tiny iron flowers woven through the bars. It hung from the ceiling on a hook above the medicine chest. Swinging inside was a perch decorated with china ivy leaves, engraved with a message long since worn away to nothing.

Scattered on the floor of the cage were a couple of thimbles, a penny covered in crumbs, and a girl under a handkerchief pretending to snore.

At midnight she sat up.

Throwing off her covers, Lily quickly crossed the birdcage. The floor swayed with her steps and the hook above creaked in the ceiling beam. Downstairs in the workshop, some of Mr. Plinker's clocks began to chime, but none of them struck twelve. They never got the hour right. It didn't matter. Lily knew what time it was—time for Escape Plan Thirty-three.

Reaching the other side of the cage, she stuck her head between the bars. The floorboards were far below. It was a long way down. She closed her eyes until the dizziness passed and looked across the room at her kidnapper. Her giant.

Gulliver had fallen asleep at his desk, like he did every night, halfway through writing one of his chapters. Lily studied him carefully. She had to be sure he really was asleep, and not just dozing.

She watched the candles on the desk as their orange flames danced to and fro with each of Gulliver's snores.

The quill was still in his hand, the Book of Travels open in front of him, but he was deep in dreams. For now.

Got to hurry, she thought.

Lily gulped half a dewdrop from one of the thimbles and rushed over to the penny, which was her plate. She scoffed down the crumbs of food, wriggled out of her nightie, and put on her dress. She had made it herself from Gulliver's silk neckerchief, stitching it together with cobwebs. The skirt and shirt she'd worn the day he snatched her from the beach was far too small now. Lily was growing up.

"Ready," she whispered to herself, kneeling by the second thimble. She put her ear to it and listened.

It was a while before she heard anything. Inside there was the faintest sound—like fingertips drumming on the metal.

"Hello, Scuttle," she murmured, for that was what she had decided to call the creature inside. "I'm sorry for trapping you all day. I had to wait, you see. Now I'm going to let you out."

Gripping the thimble with both hands, Lily readied herself. Scuttle was very fast when he was frightened. Over and over again she whispered to the creature the things she wanted him to do.

"Make sure you don't try climbing up the birdcage,

Scuttle. You want to go *down*. You want to spin a thread."

The pattering inside the thimble stopped. Scuttle was listening.

"And don't bite me, either," she murmured. "I know you're scared, but I'm not going to hurt you."

Bad thoughts spun around Lily's head then, of her gasping on the floor of the birdcage with Scuttle's poison running through her...turning purple...swelling up and going *pop*...

She shook her head, as if her worries were cobwebs in her hair. Then she pulled away the thimble with both hands to let Scuttle loose.

He wasn't there.

Lily stared wide-eyed at the space on the birdcage floor where Scuttle should have been.

"But that's impossible," she breathed. "I caught you this morning. And I just heard you moving."

Lily realized too late where the spider was. Scuttle had been hanging upside down inside the thimble. Now he was climbing out onto her shoulders.

2

Thread & Fall

Three legs—each as long as Lily's forearm—rested lightly on her sleeve. Moving just her eyes, she glanced down at them. Scuttle was halfway out of the thimble. Crouched. Watching. Very still.

His front legs prodded her arm. Could they feel her skin sweating? Her blood rushing? Her heart jump-jump-jumping in her chest? She watched for the spider's fangs, but they were hidden under what looked like a large, drooping moustache. Scuttle was the color of dirt, except for his shiny black eyes, like little globs of ink.

Suddenly he climbed out of the thimble and down her back. A trickle of sweat dribbled into Lily's eye and she blinked.

Scuttle paused. Lily didn't dare breathe.

At last he stepped lightly down her legs and dropped to the birdcage floor.

Lily was so relieved she couldn't stop the sigh. Scuttle heard. With a jolt, he sped away in terror to the far edge of the birdcage. She whirled around and saw his legs dangling in the nothingness. Then the spider found the bars of the cage and began to climb.

"No!" Lily hissed at Scuttle. "You can't climb, you've got to *fall*!"

Escape Plan Thirty-three was only seconds old and already it was going wrong! In desperation she threw the thimble, hoping to scare Scuttle back down. It spun through the air and slammed into the bars just above the spider.

There was a clang like a blacksmith's anvil and Lily looked at Gulliver, terrified he would wake. But the giant just snorted in his sleep, and that was all. When Lily turned again, Scuttle was still climbing up. She searched around desperately for something else to throw. There, by the foot of her bed were her iron shoes, rusted to two dull flakes of brown. She scooped the right one into her hands and tossed it up at Scuttle.

It flew wide, spinning through the bars and out into the attic. Another miss! Lily picked up the left. It was her last chance—Scuttle would soon be too far away. She hefted the shoe and threw it as hard as she could. It hit! The shoe struck Scuttle's front legs and the spider slipped.

He fell down and hit the floor. Lily ran forward, but Scuttle didn't get up. He didn't move at all.

He lay on his back, legs clenched; a huge, hairy fist with too many fingers. When Lily crept up to poke him with her toe, he rocked on the ground like a dry leaf. Dead.

"No," she moaned. "Oh, no. Please."

She had just wanted him to come down. She hadn't meant for this to happen. Lily backed away and slid down the bars, head in her hands. Only then did she realize that Scuttle was pretending.

Sure enough, as she watched, the spider stopped playing dead. Suddenly he wriggled his legs and righted himself. Not daring to breathe, Lily watched him crawl again to the edge of the birdcage. This time he didn't try to climb. He simply dropped down over the side and vanished.

"Good, Scuttle!" Lily leaped up and ran to where the spider had been. Down by her feet was a line of silk, fastened to the floor of the birdcage. It glinted in the light of the moon.

A lifeline. Lily's way out.

Escape Plan Thirty-three was working!

"Thank you, Scuttle," she whispered.

Sticking her head between the bars, she saw him.

Far below, the spider dangled from his silk. Down he went. Down, down, down to the dark and distant floor-boards.

Lily gripped Scuttle's thread in both hands. She took deep breaths and tried to still the jitters running through her. Her heart was thrumming in her chest, beating faster than a bee's wing. Taking one last look at her prison, she shut her eyes tight.

It was time to go home.

Squeezing sideways through the bars, she started the long climb down—suspended in the air upon a single steely thread.

Plans upon Plans

Lily climbed as quickly as she could. Scuttle's silk was not made to carry her weight. If she didn't hurry, it could snap.

And there were the breezes too.

Halfway down, the first one came. From the open window there was a whooshing sound. The ragged curtains billowed like sails. A few candles winked out on Gulliver's desk as the gust whirled in.

Lily had just enough time to wrap her legs around the silk before she was spinning around and around in the air. Then dizziness swept through her like waves and she lost her grip.

She waited for the thread to whip through her fingers; for the terrible plunge through the air; for the floorboards to rush toward her; for the final, sickening *splat*...but none of it happened. Lily stayed right where she was, fixed in place by the incredible stickiness of Scuttle's silk—it held on to her, even when she let go.

The breeze disappeared up the chimney with a moan. Lily wound her arms and legs around the thread again, holding on in case another gust came, but none did. Lily listened to Gulliver snoring. To the gentle swish of the curtains. To the glowing coals fidgeting and crumbling in the fireplace below. Then she started to climb down again. Faster.

Her hands stung and her muscles were shrieking for her to stop as Lily saw the end of the thread at last. The floorboards were just below, but there was no sign of Scuttle—he had crawled away into the shadows.

"Almost there!" she gasped, just as her arms gave out.

Lily half slid, half fell down the last few inches to the ground. The glue from the thread pulled a strip of skin from her palms, and she jolted her ankle as she hit the floorboards. She lay in a crumpled heap, groaning with the pain. Then she crawled to her feet, spat on her raw hands to kill any germs, and looked around the room.

Piles of old plates, tin cups, odd socks, and broken quills rose up around her like ruined castles. Gulliver never cleaned up after himself—he was always scribbling in his book instead. Lily looked up at him in the distance, asleep on his chair. A faraway mountain of rumbling snores.

She suddenly felt frightened, standing there all alone. In the birdcage she had been safe. Down here there could be anything lurking in the shadows. Spiders…rats… Lily shivered.

Something creaked above her. She froze, but it was just another breeze rocking the birdcage on its hook. How distant and small it looked from the floorboards, like a bell in a church tower.

Stop being so skittish.

She smiled. The first part of Escape Plan Thirty-three had worked. She had found a way out of the birdcage. Now she needed to find a way out of the attic. And then, after that…

One thing at a time, she thought, burying her worries deep down. *You won't get home until you get out of this room.*

This was harder than it sounded. Neither Gulliver nor Lily had left the attic since they'd arrived, back when the moon was a sliver. Now it was round as a coin. It was the sixth moon to pass since Gulliver had snatched her from Lilliput.

The first five moons were spent sailing on a ship. Another moon had passed here in London, in the attic above Mr. Plinker's workshop.

That was all Lily knew. She'd counted six moons wax and wane in the sky. She had listened to Mr. Plinker's clocks stutter and screech downstairs like lunatics in an asylum. Everything else was a mystery. Gulliver had kept her trapped in pockets, cages, and socks for almost the whole journey. In the attic he had hung the birdcage very carefully so that the window showed Lily nothing—just an empty square of sky that sometimes held a fleeting bird or a drifting cloud or a few distant threads of smoke.

He never told her how far they had traveled from Lilliput, or taught her about maps and the world, or let Lily even catch a glimpse of London, the city outside. She knew why. He wasn't just hiding her from the world—he was hiding the world from her.

Because the more lost and disorientated she was, the more she was his prisoner.

That was why Lily had to put all thoughts of home out of her mind for now. She couldn't look for Lilliput until she was free. Escaping Gulliver came first.

So far, though, it had not proved easy. Lily had tried thirty-two different plans and every single time she'd been caught.

During her first five Escape Plans she had tried to wriggle out of the room. To begin with, Gulliver had only concentrated on keeping Lily from climbing up the chimney, by making sure the fireplace was always filled with blazing hot coals.

Being a giant, at first he hadn't noticed all the other places Lily could squeeze through: floorboard cracks, door gaps, and keyholes.

But he had still caught her. Every time. And now every crack, gap, and keyhole was sealed up with candle wax.

So, during Escape Plan Seventeen, Lily had decided to make her own way out. Crawling into the barrel of Gulliver's pistol, she'd fetched a thimble of gunpowder from inside and blasted a hole in the floorboards. But Gulliver had woken—even though she'd stuffed fluff in his ears—and covered up the hole with a brick.

Eventually, during Escape Plan Twenty-One, Lily had decided she needed rescuing. So she had tamed a young mouse that sometimes crept in to nibble Gulliver's socks, calling him Squeak. Using a strand of giant hair, Lily tied a long scrap of paper to the mouse's tail. On it was her story, written with an eyelash and ink. It told of the Snatching on the Beach, then the long journey across the sea, and the dull days spent trapped in the attic. At the end she signed it.

Then she dipped her hand in Gulliver's ink and printed her name underneath:

Squeak had gotten away, but afterward Gulliver had stuffed his hole with poison pellets and iron wool. Lily never saw the little mouse again.

None of that mattered now, though, because the rain had stopped, the winds were calm, and Gulliver had left the window open.

"A perfect night for flying," Lily whispered.

4

Feathers & Flight

Limping over pots of old porridge, dirty clothes, and candle nubs, Lily headed for Gulliver's bed. Hidden under it, half buried in a heap of dust, were two pigeon feathers. Lily had stashed them there during Escape Plan Twenty-One. She'd planned to use them as quills for her rescue note until they proved far too big to write with.

It didn't matter. Lily had thought of another use for them.

Pulling out the feathers, she brushed off the dust and checked them over. Maybe they were a bit shabby and gray, but they were strong, and twice as tall as her.

"Come on, you two," she said to them. "Stop sitting here in the dust. I need you to fly again."

The feathers rustled and shivered in the air as if they were eager to get going. Lily felt the excitement too—it filled her with trembles. Laying down the feathers, she began turning them into wings.

First she searched in the dark for a sticky little cobweb string and untangled it. She worked as quickly as she could—there was no telling when Gulliver would wake and check on her. His nightmares never let him sleep very long. Lily could hear him now, mumbling something about giant wasps and a talking horse. There wasn't much time.

Using the spider silk, Lily bound the feathers together and made two loops on either side for her arms. When that was done she slipped in her hands and pulled the whole thing on like a backpack. She tied the last bit of cobweb around her waist to secure the feathers. Now they jutted from her shoulder blades like wings.

"Don't let me down," Lily whispered to them.

They quivered as she stepped out into the moonlight. Maybe Escape Plan Thirty-three would work.

Maybe tonight she would finally be free.

But flying out of the window would be dangerous.

The desk was the perfect place for Lily to jump—from there she could glide to the window ledge at least. But first she'd have to climb up there, and there was only one way to the top: Gulliver.

Once upon a time Lily would never have dreamed of climbing up a giant. But now she was twelve moons old. She was bigger, she was braver, and she was desperate.

Moving quickly, Lily emerged from under the bed and began scurrying up Gulliver's leg. Her palms were still raw from Scuttle's silk, and her ankle ached, but she gritted her teeth and ignored the pain. Soon she was hiking up Gulliver's shirt and tiptoeing over his back. It rose and fell with his snores. Slowly, the top of the desk came into view. The edges were piled with scraps of paper and dotted with candles, but in the center stood an enormous, leather-bound book.

It was the story of Gulliver's life—the story of his travels.

Gulliver had told Lily his tale too. As a young man, he journeyed across the world, visiting strange lands. He saw islands floating in the air, and lived with talking horses. He even visited Lilliput, long before Lily was born. But when he had returned to England, no one believed the things he had seen.

That was why, six moons ago, Gulliver went back to Lilliput.

For Lily. For proof.

Soon he was going to publish his Book of Travels. Then he would display Lily in her cage to all the giants in the city.

And everyone would know that Gulliver's travels were true.

That was why Escape Plan Thirty-three had to work. Lily was running out of time. The Book of Travels was nearly finished. When it was, every giant in the city would be staring at her and she would never be able to escape.

Tiptoeing up to Gulliver's neck, Lily slid silently down his shoulder and onto the desk. The once-tall candles were nothing but stumps now, and her feet splashed into a big pool of melted wax.

"Ouch!" she whispered, hopping from one foot to the other. "Hot, hot, hot!"

She was too busy cooling down her poor burned soles to notice one of the long feathers brush against Gulliver's nose.

The lightest touch, that's all it was.

But it was enough.

"Aaa...," said Gulliver in his sleep. "Aaa..."

5

City & Sneeze

Lily turned with dread and peered into Gulliver's huge nostrils, which were big as caves. She heard snuffling. Sniffling. Twitching. There was something inside those nostrils—something *huge*.

And it was about to come out.

"Don't you dare," she murmured at the giant's nose. "Don't you even dare."

Gulliver took a tiny breath...

Then a bigger one...

Then a huge sucking gasp that made it seem as if he was opening his mouth to swallow her up...

"*ATCHOO!*"

From Gulliver's nose, in a hurricane of snot and breath, came the sneeze. It blew out half the candles and sent a hundred scraps of paper into the air, white and tumbling. Gulliver was suddenly wide awake. He tugged his wig away from his eyes and whirled around.

"Lily?" he rumbled, looking at the birdcage.

"Lily!" he roared, looking down at his desk.

"Lily!" he raged in the whirlwind of paper. He turned to the open window. "Lily! Lily, where are you?"

But Lily was gone.

Gulliver's sneeze had caught in her wings with the force of a gale and blown her off the desk into nothingness.

For a moment she hung in the air with the moonbeams and the paper scraps...then she was spinning, soaring, flying out the window.

I've done it! I'm free!

With the wind in her hair, the starry sky above her head, and the moon within her reach, Lily stretched out her arms and swooped out of the attic. And, at last, she caught her first glimpse of the city called London.

She gasped.

Vast plumes of smoke came up from the chimneys, smudging the stars. All around, the tiled rooftops stretched out to the horizon like the peaks of mountains. Lily could not believe her eyes. The city was enormous. An endless tangle of streets. A hundred thousand windows glimmering under the moon.

She tried to focus on flying, but it was impossible. Lily had never imagined anything could be this big. For so long her world had been small. It had boundaries. The walls of an attic. The bars of a birdcage. The inside of a pocket. But London had no limits—it was endless.

Where do I go now?

Which way is home?

For a moment Lily hesitated, pulling on her wings. She hovered in the air. Just for a moment.

And back inside the attic, Gulliver saw his chance.

With a desperate lunge he launched himself half out of the window. His hand rushed down toward her and his fingertips closed around the tip of one wing. Before Lily could wriggle free of the knots that tied her to the feathers, he yanked her back inside.

The moon and stars and city suddenly vanished. There was a *slam* as the window swung shut. When Lily

sat up, giddy and shaken, she was on Gulliver's hand, staring up at his face.

"You are not a bird, Lily," he said once he had caught his breath. "And so it is foolish of you to try and fly away."

As he spoke he began pulling off her wings. Lily couldn't stop him. She didn't even try. She said nothing; just covered her face with her hands as if she could press the hot tears back into her eyes.

And, as the knots of cobweb stretched and snapped, Lily felt something stretching and snapping inside her too. Whatever threads had been pulling her closer to home, they were broken now.

6

Gulliver & His Lectures

Gulliver tossed the feathers into the fireplace where they shriveled up on the coals. Lily couldn't bear to watch them burn. She looked up at his face, full of creases and lines, like a map that had been folded and unfolded too many times.

"I am tired of this, Lily," he grumbled above her. "Again and again you try. How many times do I have to catch you?"

Lily almost answered. She almost said, *None, Gulliver. You won't have to catch me any more. I'm stopping. I'm giving up.*

"You would do better to forget Lilliput and make a new home here," he said, taking off his spectacles and rubbing his eyes. "In London."

He was right. How could she keep going? There were no more escape plans, no more hope. Even if Lily freed herself she would still have to find a way out of

London. It was impossible. Lilliput was lost, somewhere beyond the horizon, out of reach.

But then Lily remembered. For a brief, wonderful second, she had been flying. She had been *free*.

And even though Lilliput now seemed farther away than ever—even though Scuttle was gone, Gulliver was awake, and the window was shut—Lily still remembered that feeling.

It was enough.

"I won't stop," she said quietly, surprised by her own words. But the more she spoke, the more she believed. "I won't give up. I'll keep trying to escape until I'm free."

"Nonsense!" said Gulliver hotly. "Absurd! Once you escape, what then? London is enormous—you have seen that for yourself now. And it is filled with dangers. Do I need to remind you of the fate of those I brought back from my first voyage to Lilliput? Do I need to show you their bones once more?"

Lily shivered and shook her head. Gulliver still kept the skeletons of the Lilliputian cows and sheep he had brought back from the island after his first journey. Every now and then he took them out to show her what would happen if she ever succeeded in running away.

"I let them graze in a field in Greenwich," he began, though Lily had heard the story many times before. "Within a week the rats had gobbled up every single one.

I found their bones scattered over the grass. Picked clean. Don't you see, Lily? I am not keeping you prisoner—I am keeping you safe."

Once, when she was younger, the story of the bones had been terrifying. But Lily was twelve moons old now and it no longer scared her. She knew why.

"I'd rather be a rat's supper than your proof," she said.

Gulliver looked at her sternly, and she glared back. There was stubble on his chin, bags under his eyes, and snuff on his nose. Several sentences from his *Book of Travels* were printed upon his forehead from where he'd been sleeping. In the same way, his dream of horses was still smudged upon his eyes. Lily could see it as it galloped out of his head.

Giant eyes were not like Lilliputian eyes. They were so huge that sometimes, if she looked hard enough, Lily saw Gulliver's feelings. His thoughts. He tried his best to keep them locked away, but every now and then one would get free.

Lily saw one escape now.

"I don't belong here," she told him. "You know I don't—I can see it in your eyes."

Gulliver blinked behind his spectacles and hid his thoughts away again. "It is nothing to do with right and wrong."

"Yes it is," she insisted, and tried explaining it in the smallest, simplest way she could. "You stole me. Stealing is wrong."

Gulliver shook his head. "Yet again it seems I must explain." He sighed, blowing her long black curls from her eyes. "Keeping you here is necessary, Lily. Perhaps I am foolish to expect something so small to under-stand—"

"Hey!" She thumped his palm with her fists. "I'm not a something, I'm a *someone*."

His enormous cheeks blushed.

"And don't ever call me small, either," she growled. "You're big."

Gulliver tried his best to smile kindly.

"Lily...," he began, but she shook her head and stuck her fingers in her ears. "Lily, listen."

Gulliver was about to embark on another one of his lectures. He did it at least once every day. Taking her in his palm—and using words like *reason* and *sensible* and *scientific progress*—he would patiently try to convince Lily that he wasn't an evil kidnapping giant at all.

And perhaps, Lily thought, he was trying to con-vince himself too.

"You must understand, Lily," he began, like a teacher giving a lesson. "I am not a kidnapper; I am a man of science and reason. And you are not my prisoner, as you just said yourself. You are my proof. The proof of all my travels!"

Lily closed her eyes. She had heard this speech before. It was always the same. Now he was gesturing to his book.

"In this country, no one else has been to the places I have been, or seen the things I have seen."

He counted them off on his gigantic fingers.

"They do not know about Laputa, the floating island. They do not know about the *struldbrugs*, the immortals from the East. They do not even know about Lilliput—your old home—and all of its miniature inhabitants."

"Yes," said Lily. "And I hope it stays that way. The last thing Lilliput needs is you giants stomping all over it."

And she stuck her fingers in her ears and began to hum.

"Do not say that," said Gulliver. His voice was so rumbling and deep that Lily could not help but hear him. "London, and the rest of the world, must be enlightened. It must know the truth. That is why I need you, Lily. Without you no one will believe me. Without proof my *Book of Travels* will seem like a fantastical story...a story for children!"

Lily scrunched up her face in disgust. This was the worst part. This was what made her feel sick with fury.

"No one has ever taken my writing seriously. That is why I brought you here to London. Do you see how precious you are? People will only believe me if they can see you."

Lily shook her head bitterly. All Gulliver wanted was for people to buy his book. He might talk about truth and reason, but really he had kidnapped her out of greed.

"It is the only way," Gulliver continued. "Believe me. Eighteen years ago I came back from my first journey to Lilliput—"

Lily groaned. "I've heard this all a hundred times."

"Then you must hear it again!" Gulliver snapped. "I will tell you until you understand. After my first journey to Lilliput I went straight to Parliament and told them I had visited a nation of tiny people. They thought I was crazy! I very narrowly escaped being locked up in the asylum!"

"I wish they had locked you up," muttered Lily. "Then you'd know what it feels like. Then you'd let me free."

Gulliver ignored her. "Curse those politicians! What yahoos!"

"Yahoo" was Gulliver's name for other giants. He had learned it on one of his travels, when he met a race of talking horses. The talking horses had taught Gulliver that human beings were cruel creatures—as savage as apes. Ever since then he had called other people yahoos, just like the horses did.

Sometimes Lily wondered whether Gulliver had forgotten that he was also a yahoo himself.

"Yahoos, everywhere I look!" he shouted in a rage. "All I want is for them to know the truth!"

Gulliver ground his teeth together and went to drive a fist into his palm in indignation, only stopping when he realized that would squash Lily flat. He stared at her. His eyes were bloodshot and full of doubt.

"I have always looked after you well, Lily." He was a little out of breath. "I have fed you. Protected you. Civilized you. Taught you to speak English, to read and write. And, yes, when you have misbehaved, I have punished you."

Lily began to tremble. For a moment she thought Gulliver was going to stick her in the Sock. But he just sighed and sat her down on the desk by the candles.

"But I am not a yahoo," he said, "and so I will keep you from your cage. For the rest of tonight you may stay here, where I can keep an eye on you."

Lily turned away. She sat with her legs dangling off the edge of the desk, staring at the floorboards below.

"Be patient, Lily," he said gently. "I have a few final

chapters to write. When I am finished I will show you and my book to King George himself. Then you will understand. You will forget this silly idea about going home. Your home will be here instead, and you will live like a princess, adored by everyone!"

Lily said nothing. She watched Gulliver pick up his scattered notes from the floor. He reordered them, dipped his quill in ink, and began to write again.

The closer he gets to finishing that book, she thought, *the farther I am from home.*

7

Slubber & Stunkle

L ily warmed her hands by a lit candle. She looked at Gulliver as he scribbled and yawned.

Sooner or later, he'll fall asleep, and I'll think of a new escape plan. All I have to do is wait.

So Lily sat watching her kidnapper to see if his eyes were drooping. But he drank cups of yesterday's coffee to keep from sleep. Maybe all the Escape Plans were trapped somewhere, just like she was. Hours passed, and nothing came.

For a long time the only sounds were Gulliver scratching away with his quill and the coals shifting in the fireplace. Outside, the street was silent. A horse neighed in the stables across the road. In Mr. Plinker's workshop downstairs, a broken clock was stubbornly chiming thirteen.

"What are you doing?" Gulliver said as he scribbled. His eyes did not leave the paper.

"Thinking," said Lily shortly.

"Good," said Gulliver. "Perhaps you will reflect on the error of your ways. Perhaps you will realize how necessary it is that you help instead of hinder me."

Lily scowled at him. Her hopes were low, her patience was thin and her temper was short. She was trapped—again—and Gulliver was explaining—again—how everything was necessary.

It was one of those intensely irritating and painful moments—like Gulliver's spontaneous trigonometry lessons—which could only be made better by shouting lots of bad words.

The only problem was Lily didn't know any. Not in English. Gulliver had only taught her polite words so that when the time came she would be able to entertain giant princes and answer the queries of giant scientists.

Luckily, Lily knew plenty of bad words in Lilliputian.

"Oh, be quiet, you *flustian mungle boff*," she muttered.

Gulliver stopping his scribbling and pointed a warning finger at her. He hated it when Lily talked in Lilliputian. Especially when she called him such rude things.

"You," he said, "are very vulgar."

Lily sat back and grinned. "And you are a *slubber*, and your *stunkles eek* like an *uckbluck!*"

Gulliver's mouth dropped open. His spectacles slid

a little way down his nose. "That is completely untrue!" he cried. "My armpits do not smell remotely like a—"

"Oh, why don't you go and flimbip a boffybumf on its nozzer?" Lily giggled.

"How dare you?" he cried, blushing. "I would never be so disgusting as to kiss something like that! I would probably catch all sorts of infections—"

"Be quiet, you quog!" Lily shouted. She went over to the candles and wrote more bad words in the spilled wax. "You zijji guncher!"

"Behave yourself!" he thundered. "Speak properly!"

"I won't!" said Lily, dancing across his desk. She jumped up onto his ink bottle, dipped her feet inside, and started to tread black footprints all across his *Book of Travels*. "You can't make me!"

Gulliver tore his hair in exasperation. "Where did you learn this foul language, child?" he cried, blotting the stains on his paper.

"Not from you," said Lily, and then she paused and suddenly blurted out: "You *yahoo*! That's right! You're the biggest, meanest, cruelest yahoo of all!"

And with that she kicked a candle so hard, it toppled right over and fell onto the *Book of Travels*.

The flame caught on a dog-eared page and suddenly it seemed to Lily like the whole desk was on fire. The pages of the book shriveled to ash as she staggered backward, horrified and awestruck by what she had done.

Above her came an ear-splitting shriek. She looked up at Gulliver, his eyes relfecting the flames. With one hand, he snatched Lily away from the fire. Then he grabbed the iron kettle from the hearth and tipped it over the desk. A great waterfall of dirty brown coffee poured from the spout. Lily gasped and shut her eyes.

The coffee hit the Book of Travels with a sizzling sound. The flames vanished, the candles winked out, and a billow of steam rushed past Lily and up to the ceiling.

In the sudden darkness Gulliver opened his mouth to try and speak. His eyes began to water. His palm trembled. It was as if Lily had suddenly grown many times her size and struck him a terrible blow.

"My work...," he managed at last. "My book...my travels..."

Lily nervously tugged at the giant's sleeve. She had gone too far and she knew it. "I'm sorry," she said, trying to wriggle out of the trouble she was in. "You're not really a yahoo."

But Gulliver just stared at the mass of pulp and ash on his desk. Only a few pages had burned away completely, but there were hundreds that were now singed, or soaked, or coffee-stained.

"Are you going to punish me?" Lily asked in a small, shaking voice.

Gulliver was now purple with rage. The hand she sat on began to clench into a fist.

Lily was afraid.

"Please don't put me in the Sock," she pleaded as his fingers closed around her like the bars of a cage. "Please, Gulliver. I said I was sorry. Don't put me in the Sock. Don't put me in there."

Lily turned and crawled under Gulliver's sleeve, but he plucked her out with his other hand. She kicked, she screamed, she dangled from his fingers as he carried her over to where the Sock hung on a rusty nail by the door.

Lily said "Don't" over and over again. She said "No" and "Please" and "I'm sorry."

He didn't listen. He dropped her. She fell.

Down into the darkness of the Sock.

8

Sock & Story

Whenever one of Lily's Escape Plans broke, burned, or blew up something they shouldn't have, Gulliver stuffed her in the Sock. It was the itchiest, smelliest thing that Gulliver owned. After an hour squirming around inside it, Lily would emerge all splotchy, sweaty, and stinking, like some horrible variety of cheese.

But the prickly, itchy wool and old, sweaty smell weren't the worst things about the Sock. The worst thing was that it was also infested with fleas. And London's fleas, like everything else in the city, were gigantic.

They bounced all over Lily's skin, as big as marbles, looking for a place to bite. She had to flick them away before they bit.

This was why the Sock was so horrible. If Lily stayed still, the fleas nibbled on her. But if she moved around, it was like dancing inside a holly bush. And no matter what she did, there would always be the suffocating stink of Gulliver's giant feet. If she breathed through her nose she smelled them. If she breathed through her mouth she *tasted* them.

And so, as Lily landed in the Sock, she immediately began to itch, and flick, and retch. It was awful. It was torture. But luckily, over the moons, Lily had learned how to escape from the Sock. In a way. For a little while.

From the second Gulliver dumped her in to the moment he shook her out, Lily told herself stories. Memories. Scraps of her life before the Snatching.

They might be funny stories (like "When the Seagull Pooped on Nana") or sad stories (like "When the Rains Washed Mama and Papa Away"). Lily told the funny stories to take her mind off the itching and biting. She told the sad stories so she'd always remember—worse things had happened to her than being trapped in the Sock.

This time Lily pretended she was home in Lilliput. She imagined the whole village sitting on the beach, with the sky dark and the tide out and everyone snuggled up cozy by the fires, begging her to tell them a story of her adventures among the giants.

Lily closed her eyes. What could she say to them? What adventures were there to tell? None. Just six dull moons spent in cages, pockets, and socks. Just thirty-three Escape Plans, each one ending in failure.

No, wait, she told herself. *There is one story.*

"I saved a giant's life once," Lily whispered. "On the day we arrived in London. I'll tell how it happened. It isn't a funny story, though. It isn't sad, either. It's gruesome. Listen..."

And, gathering up everything she had heard and seen on that night and the nights since, Lily began to speak aloud.

9

Clock & Stitch

"Once on a winding street," Lily began, "lived the most cruel clock maker in the whole city. His name was Mr. Plinker. Altogether he had built hundreds of clocks, and none of them worked.

"His pocket watches ran fast. His grandfather clocks ran slow. His mantel clocks ran forward or backward, depending on the day of the week.

"Every now and again one of them would explode.

"That's right.

"*Explode!*

"Mr. Plinker's clocks were so poorly made, so terribly treated, and so horribly overpriced that they were dangerous as well as useless. At least, that's what I heard his customers yell whenever they came back to the workshop to complain.

"Mr. Plinker blamed the clocks, but it wasn't their

fault. They were the victims, and Mr. Plinker was their tormentor.

"He nailed them to the wall above the counter.

"He pulled them apart in his workshop.

"He tried selling them to rich gentlemen.

"Then, if that failed, he would twist off their hands and smash their faces, and when at last they could tick no more, he threw them in the fireplace and began the whole horrible process again on another victim.

"I heard everything from my birdcage in the attic. I knew that Mr. Plinker didn't make clocks.

"He tortured them.

"And so, of course, it was only a matter of time before one of them tried to murder him."

Now Lily paused and smiled, imagining the gasps of horror from her audience. They would be hooked. Hanging on her every word. Inside the Sock it seemed as if even the fleas had stopped their nibbling to sit and listen.

"Have you ever heard of such a thing?" she whispered. "A clock that tried to murder its maker?

"Well, I'll tell you something even stranger about that clock. Its name was the 'Astronomical Budgerigar.'

"The Astronomical Budgerigar was Mr. Plinker's own kind of cuckoo clock. It was tall and square, with a

51

little triangular roof and a glass window above the clock face. It looked like a Lilliputian-sized house. Every hour, when the big hand pointed straight up, a perch shot out of the clock on a spring, and a bird sitting on it called out the time.

"But what made the Astronomical Budgerigar different—what made it cruel and evil—was that Mr. Plinker hadn't put a pretend bird inside the clock. He had put a real one there instead.

"A live bird, trapped in a mechanical cage."

Lily paused again. That would be too much for some of the older Lilliputians. *A live bird, inside a clock?* They wouldn't be able to imagine it. They would gasp and shake their heads in disbelief.

"Maybe you don't believe me, but it's true," she went on. "I know. I saw it with my own eyes. I was there, in the workshop, the night that it was made. Gulliver took me out from his pocket and put me on Mr. Plinker's counter. I stood staring up at that terrible clock, and I heard the poor creature inside, calling out for help. I wanted to set it free so badly, but I couldn't. I was a prisoner too.

"And, besides, the trapped bird wasn't the only one who needed my help.

"Because I could see Mr. Plinker lying in front of me, and he was dying.

"I don't know how it had happened exactly. I don't want to know. It's too horrible to think about. But it isn't hard to imagine, is it? Clocks are like staircases, or jigsaws. They're not usually dangerous, but if you leave them lying around unfinished, terrible accidents can happen.

"Mr. Plinker had probably been busy tinkering, with his hands deep inside the Astronomical Budgerigar. Perhaps his fingers had brushed the wrong pulley or lever, and somehow the murderous clock had started to tick.

"Before Mr. Plinker could take out his hand the cogs began to grind, spokes began to stab, pistons began to pound. So he jerked his fingers free.

"Most of them, anyway.

"Then he had fainted on his counter as if it was his coffin, looking as pale as death. That's where I first saw him.

"I turned around. I didn't want to look. I've seen blood before, but this was different. There was a whole river of red, flooding from his hand, all over the counter. I looked up at Gulliver. I almost wished he'd kept me in his pocket.

"'Don't worry,' he told me. 'I have given Mr. Plinker several sleeping drops.' Gulliver pointed at a brown glass bottle in his hand. 'He is deep in his dreams, and I have sent his apprentice up to bed. No one will see you.'

"'Why are we here?' I gasped.

"'Because Mr. Plinker's apprentice was wandering the streets, looking for a doctor to mend his master,' Gulliver answered. 'And he found me. And, because I am a doctor, I agreed to follow him back here and save Mr. Plinker's life. For a price.'

"'What price?' I asked him, and Gulliver told me, looking very pleased with himself as he did so.

"'Mr. Plinker is going to let us stay in his attic, for as long as we wish. Do you not realize our good fortune, Lily? Two hours ago our ship sailed into London, and already I have found us a place to stay. Somewhere I can finish my Book of Travels, and keep you safe. All we have to do now is save Mr. Plinker's life, quickly.'

"As Gulliver spoke he left me on the counter, next to Mr. Plinker and his awful clock, and began to move around the room, gathering things. It was the dead of night, only one sickly candle burned, and even my sharp eyes could not see what he was collecting.

"'How do we save his life?' I asked.

"Gulliver smiled and showed me the things in his palm: a splinter of wood and a tangle of spider silk.

"'I can't save him, Lily,' he said. 'I am old, and my fingers are clumsy. But you can do it. With your nimble fingers and sharp eyesight you can stitch him back together.'

"At first I just laughed. 'I'll never help you, you non-dongling nunnerbutt,' I said.

"But Gulliver smiled. 'You won't be helping me,' he said. 'You will be helping this man. And if you don't, he will die.'

"'He won't,' I said, looking at Mr. Plinker's mangled hand and the sticky red around it. 'Giants have oceans of blood. He's only lost a lake's worth.'

"'That doesn't matter,' said Gulliver. 'If you don't stitch him back together then an infection will creep into the wound, and he will catch a fever and die. When he dies, his apprentice—who is only a boy—will be homeless. He has a cat too. Without an owner to look after them they will probably starve.'

"I looked across at the clock maker as he whimpered in his sleep, and even though I was seeing him for the first time...even though I didn't know then just how nasty Mr. Plinker was, he still sent a shiver up my spine.

"But that didn't matter. Mr. Plinker was dying, and I could save his life. If I refused, it would make me a murderer. And a murderer is one of the worst things you can be. Even worse than a kidnapper.

"'I'll do it,' I said at last to Gulliver. 'Not for you. Not for Mr. Plinker, either. But for his apprentice. And his cat.'

"So I stepped onto Gulliver's palm. I picked up the splinter. I threaded it with the spider silk, then sat down by Mr. Plinker's mangled hand. As quickly as I could, I started to sew.

"That's how I saved Mr. Plinker's life. And that's how we ended up in his attic too," Lily finished.

10

Seventeen Steps & a Stranger

As Lily finished her story, the imaginary crowds of listening Lilliputians faded away. She was still in the Sock. Still trapped. She waited for Gulliver to take pity and let her out. Nothing happened. The itching and the smell and the fleas carried on.

Her story hadn't changed anything, but it had helped. For a little while.

So Lily took a deep breath and told it again. Two hundred and twenty times she told the story of Mr. Plinker and his murderous clock. Over and over she repeated it, until her throat was sore.

The first one hundred times the story was a way to escape Gulliver's prison. Lily imagined herself telling the story to Lilliputian crowds all across the island—to the fishermen at the Plips minnow market, to the crowds of passersby at Lilliput's capital of Mildendo, and even to the Emperor Himself at the Imperial Palace at Belfaborac.

But eventually that grew boring.

The second hundred times the story became a way for Lily to let Gulliver know how furious she was with him. She embellished her tale with unflattering descriptions of his silly spectacles and wrinkled face. The moment she called him a *nondongling nunnerbut* became a whole torrent of insults.

But eventually insulting Gulliver became boring too.

So, for the final twelve times, Lily spoke just to remind Gulliver that she was still there. She spoke to stop him forgetting.

Though the Sock was far too thick for Lily to see through, its coarse wool did let in the color of the light. And so it was that she saw the moonbeams tarnish, from silver to steel to rusted iron.

She saw the sky outside turn from black to bruise-blue to pink, and heard birds begin to sing.

And still Gulliver left her there.

Dawn came.

Though he had punished her before, Gulliver had never left her in the Sock for so long. Lily had always considered herself too precious for him to hurt in any way. Now, for the first time, she realized how helpless she was. How completely in his power.

On and on her punishment went, on and on without end. Lily became frightened. She didn't know how much more she could bear. But, at last, something rescued her from the monotony of bites, itches, stinks, and start-again stories.

It wasn't Gulliver.

It was a smell; the smell of breakfast wafting up the stairs.

Lily gasped. The smell was so rich, so delicious, and so unexpected that, for a moment, she almost fainted. Then a flea jumped up and nipped her, right in her armpit, and she yelped and came to again.

Oh! Lily thought, cold tears on her raw cheeks. *Breakfast! Surely Gulliver will let me out now, I haven't eaten in hours!*

Breakfast was always porridge and coffee. It arrived every morning at six. It came in a bowl and a mug, which Gulliver would then decant into thimbles for Lily. He paid Mr. Plinker sixpence a day to bring breakfast up the staircase and leave it on the landing by the attic door.

Mr. Plinker had never come inside, and Lily had only seen him once, on the night she saved his life. But though she never saw the clock maker, Lily still knew when he was bringing up the breakfast because of the racket he made.

Giants made so much noise that it was very difficult for Lily not to hear them. Even when Mr. Plinker tried his best to tiptoe up the stairs, she knew he was there from the stomp-squelch of his heart and the bubble-boil of his blood and the rattle-wheeze of his lungs.

There was also the smell. Mr. Plinker stank of rot and swamps. The clock maker could always be identified by his farts, which came out in great gut-tearing torrents, as if his trousers had ripped.

Usually when he came up the stairs Lily was torn between holding her nose and covering her ears. But not this time. This time something very strange was happening.

For the first time ever, the person now outside on the landing was absolutely *not* Mr. Plinker.

It was somebody else.

A stranger.

Even inside the sweaty Sock, Lily could tell that this stranger was different. He smelled of brass and polish. He sounded different too. His blood didn't bubble-boil, it river-rushed; his heart didn't stomp-squelch, it quiver-clenched.

And there were other clues.

Mr. Plinker always tiptoed up the seventeen stairs as softly as he could. Then, he knelt on the landing every morning (knees making a sound like pencils snapping), and did his best to eavesdrop on Gulliver.

Then, after straining his ears at the blocked-up key-hole, the clock maker would—without fail—clunk the porridge and coffee down. Then he'd get to his feet and tap-tap-tap his shoe impatiently for Gulliver to call out "Many thanks" and push a sixpence under the door.

The stranger—whoever it was—could hardly have been more different. Lily heard him clomp up the stairs, lay out the breakfast, and then clomp back down again.

No eavesdropping.

No foot-tapping.

He was there, and then he was gone. Or was he?

Inside the Sock, Lily felt something else gnaw away at her, and unless she had accidentally swallowed a flea she didn't know what it could be. Something else wasn't right. Something else had been different.

She racked her brains. Clomping up the stairs, no eavesdropping, no foot-tapping, clomping back down again... What else?

All at once she realized. That was it! Mr. Plinker always climbed seventeen steps up and down the stairs. Lily counted the stranger's steps back down the stairs—he had stopped at twelve.

So whoever it was hadn't gone away. He was still five steps from the bottom of the stairs, waiting.

Waiting for what?

11

Coffee & Sorry

Gulliver's chair scraped on the floor as he rose from his desk. He pulled open the door. Lily's stomach lurched as the Sock swung on its nail.

"Gulliver," she whimpered, knowing that he was close enough to hear. "Let me out. Please, let me out."

Outside the Sock, Gulliver hesitated. Lily felt him wavering.

"Let me out," she pleaded. "I'll tell you a secret."

She heard him sigh as he put a sixpence on the landing, gathered up the breakfast, and shut the door. Then the Sock suddenly lifted off its nail, the world turned on its head, and Lily was falling. She tumbled out, bounced upon Gulliver's bed, and plowed into a twist of bedsheets.

There she lay in a heap, gasping with relief. Her whole body ached and stung, but at least now the air was fresh and cool, and wasn't full of fleas. It was heaven.

Looking up, she saw Gulliver watching.

"I have rewritten the pages you burned," he said. "The damage was…not as bad as I first thought."

She didn't answer. He fetched two thimbles, one of porridge and one of coffee, and placed them on the mattress beside her.

"I am sorry, Lily," he said. "I fear I punished you too harshly. It was not fair. But I was angry, and I…I did something that comes very naturally to us yahoos—I was cruel. I won't do it again, ever."

And he threw the Sock into the fireplace.

As it smoldered and burned on the coals, Lily staggered to her feet and gave Gulliver her best glare. He did look very sorry, but that didn't mean she forgave him. It didn't mean she was sorry for scorching his *Book of Travels*, either.

"Eat, Lily," said Gulliver, slurping on his porridge. "Drink."

Her stomach rumbled and her throat was dry as dust, but Lily pushed the thimbles away with her toe.

"Talk to me," he pleaded. "Just now you said you would tell me a secret. Well, go on. I'm listening."

Lily opened her mouth, then clamped it shut again. Why should she tell him about the stranger on the stairs? It would mean she had forgiven him, and she hadn't. He needed to be tormented. Just a little. She wanted to punish him, for punishing her.

"Lily," he said miserably. "Please, Lily. I do not like to think of you being unhappy here. I want you—no, I want us—to work together. To tell the world the truth."

He edged the coffee forward with the tip of his little finger. She pushed it away again with her foot.

"But you must drink," he said, draining his cup dry. "You must eat. You must look after yourself. It is necessary."

Lily narrowed her eyes, crossed her arms, and shook her head.

Gulliver blinked at her slowly. "Aren't you tired?" he asked. "I am exhausted. Surely some coffee would make you feel better." He rubbed his eyes. "I think I need another cup myself."

He yawned and fetched the coffee pot. He poured it out, but missed his cup completely.

"*Ouch!*" he hissed as the hot drink sloshed over his hand. He fumbled in his pockets for a handkerchief, brought one out, and dropped it.

Reaching down to pick it up, he somehow fell off his chair.

Thump!

Lily laughed. Her laugh faded to a frown. Gulliver wasn't getting back up. On her hands and knees, she crawled across the bed and peered over the edge.

Gulliver lay on the floor, blinking stupidly.

"Pardon?" he said.

"I didn't say anything," said Lily. "Why are you lying on the floor?"

Gulliver stared at her in utter bewilderment. "But I am not lying on the floor," he said after a moment. "*You* are lying on the ceiling!"

Lily was now quite confused herself. What was he talking about? Gulliver was sweating, sweating all over, and he wiped his head with his arm.

"What is wrong with me?" he gasped. "What have you done?"

With one arm he clutched feebly at his coffee mug. He raised it to his nose and sniffed.

"Sleeping drops!" His eyes bulged, and in them Lily saw him think of something: a brown glass bottle. "You...you drugged me with my own medicine!"

Lily was astonished. Had she done that? Sleeping drops in Gulliver's coffee certainly sounded like one of her

Escape Plans—and a very good one too. It was just that she couldn't remember doing it. But if it not her, who?

Then she remembered the stranger on the stairs.

"How?" Gulliver rasped, trying to lift himself from the floor. "I left the sleeping drops...on Mr. Plinker's counter...the night you stitched him back together... How did you get hold of them?"

"I didn't," Lily insisted. "It wasn't me, it was..." But she couldn't say, because she didn't know.

"Lily, don't leave me," Gulliver gasped. "What about...progress? What about...truth? What about...?" Drool spilled over his lips and onto his chin.

Then his eyes rolled back into his head and he started snoring like a baby.

Lily stared down at the giant in shock. Then she leaped into the air as if struck by lightning. There was a *thump, thump, thump* coming up the stairs.

The stranger!

She had to find somewhere to hide!

The quilt on Gulliver's bed was one big twist and tangle; all piled up on itself like a gigantic sloppy wedding cake. Lily spotted a fold and ran toward it as the stranger's steps grew louder, closer...

Come on, Lily! Wriggle your way in!

The stranger was on the landing.

Hurry! Get your legs in too!

The doorknob turned.

Don't get seen.

The door swung open.

Quick!

With a final kick, Lily squirmed inside the quilt. She lay there, gasping for breath and listening. Someone was there. But who? Not daring to make a sound, she peeked out of the quilt fold and saw him.

Another giant.

A boy.

"Lily?" he said. "Lily, are you there?"

12

Quilts & Questions

L ily was flabbergasted. The boy in the doorway was talking to her. He knew her name.

She shook her head, because that was impossible. She was Gulliver's secret, his prisoner, his prized possession. No other giant in London knew Lily even existed. Yet the boy stood in the doorway and spoke to her again.

"I got your note, Lily," he said. "Look."

The boy wore a grimy waistcoat. He took a scrap of paper from its pocket. His fingers unfolded it nimbly and held it out to the room.

"See?" he said. "Here."

Peeking out of the fold in the quilt, Lily squinted and saw.

On the scrap of paper were words. Her words. The story she had written with an eyelash, a dozen nights and plans ago, and signed:

LILY

She was amazed. The last time she'd seen her story it had been tied to Squeak's tail. It *worked*, she thought numbly. *After all this time, Escape Plan Twenty-one actually worked. This boy found my note!*

Lily almost jumped out there and then, shouting, "I'm here, I'm here, what took you so long?"

But she stopped herself. Squeak might have trusted this boy with her story, but Lily still had too many questions. Who was he? Where had he come from? What would he do now?

She searched the boy's blue eyes for an answer, trying to see if his thoughts were there, but he stood too far away.

"Lily?" he whispered, creeping farther into the room. "Lily, you must be here somewhere. Where are you?"

But Lily kept quiet. Hidden in the quilt folds, she studied his thick black hair, his skin tinged pink, his fingertips stained with oil and scars. She remembered what Gulliver had said, about the giants not realizing how big they were.

He's taller than a house, she thought, *but he thinks he's small.*

That gave her a good feeling. Now she was beginning to see why Squeak had trusted this boy with her story.

Should she take a chance and trust him too?

I want to, she told herself.

"You have to come out, Lily," said the boy desperately. "We don't have long."

He looked down anxiously. There was a watch attached to his wrist and it was ticking.

He's Mr. Plinker's apprentice, Lily realized suddenly. *The one who found Gulliver when the clock maker was hurt. The one who brought us here.*

"Please, Lily," the boy whispered. "We're wasting time."

As if in agreement, the watch buckled around his wrist went *ding-dong*, and the boy hissed in pain and clutched his arm.

Lily stared at the watch in shock. It was sharp-edged, the color of rusted iron. The clock face was a warped oval, with a single jagged hand. It was attached by a leather strap that coiled around the boy's wrist. There was no buckle. No way to loosen it.

It's on far too tight, Lily thought. *Why doesn't he just take it off?*

A chilling idea came: *Maybe he can't.*

Lily bit her lip. She flitted between trust and doubt like a bird between branches—the boy seemed kind, but what about his watch? It looked just like one of Mr. Plinker's inventions. Cruel.

70

Evil.

"Lily?" said the boy, rubbing the pain at his wrist. "You don't have to hide. I'm not here to hurt you. I found your note...well, Horatio found it really, but I snatched it from him."

The last bit of Lily's good feeling disappeared. So the boy hadn't found her note at all. He had stolen it from someone else. What if he was here to snatch her too?

"I was tinkering in the workshop," the boy babbled on in a whisper. "Horatio came up the stairs to have his lunch. He'd caught a mouse. Luckily he always plays with his food, and the little thing managed to get away before Horatio could gobble him up."

Lily recoiled in horror. Poor Squeak! So he hadn't trusted a giant at all—instead he'd been caught and almost eaten! She felt sick. Gulliver had told her that all yahoos were savage and cruel, but until now she'd never quite believed him.

"I chased Horatio back down the stairs, and that's when I saw it—the tip of a mouse's tail, left on the step. Horatio must have chopped it off with his claws. And wrapped around the tail was your note."

Lily wanted to burst into tears. She wanted to scream and shout. She wanted to find this horrible Horatio and chop him up into bits, to see how he liked it. But she couldn't. She had to stay still.

She closed her eyes and sent a little prayer up to the Ender. For Squeak. Her brave little half-tailed mouse. Then she thought about what to do next. She had a choice to make.

Lily looked at the boy. What did she know about him?

He snatches things. His friend is a torturer. He works for cruel Mr. Plinker.

What would a boy like that do to Lily if he found her?

He might put her in a jar with wasps, and watch.

Or sell her to a circus freak show.

Or bleed her dry with leeches, and dissect her like a toad.

Suddenly Lily decided not to wriggle out of the quilt but to burrow farther in. She would hide from this boy with his jagged watch and his fingers full of scars.

I'll wait until he goes. Then I can escape on my own.

She squirmed her way deeper into the folds and creases. Very soon it was pitch-black— there was nothing but the smell of goose feathers and sweat.

Still she went deeper, through twisting, folding passageways. Lily imagined the boy creeping around the attic, peering into the birdcage, checking under the bed.

At last, when it was so stuffy she couldn't bear to

go any farther, Lily stopped and tried to listen. The quilt muffled everything except her own gasps and heartbeat. Had he gone? Was she safe?

Around her the quilt began to move.

Suddenly all the creases and folds rippled and smoothed out, and Lily tumbled around and around. The quilt opened up like a crumpled white envelope and she fell out on to the bed.

The boy stood above her. He threw the quilt to the floor and his head angled down, and he saw her.

He saw Lily.

13

Eye to Eye

With a yelp, the boy stepped back into the breakfast bowl. He slipped in the porridge, yelped again, and fell to the floor with a crash. Then he was still.

Lily peered over the side of the bed. The boy lay there like a fallen tree.

"I've killed him," she whispered, not quite knowing how she'd done it.

Suddenly the boy groaned. His eyes flickered open and fixed on Lily again. This time he didn't blink, he stared. Lily saw her own reflection in his eyes: a tiny girl with silk-slippered feet, in a dress of cobwebs and silk. Hair so black and fine it was a wisp of smoke. Eyes shining like dew drops.

She had a dozen different thoughts then. Some said run, and others said *hide*, and one very brave and very stupid thought said *fight*.

But in the end Lily ignored them all. Before she could run or hide or fight her eyes became blurs, her legs turned to trembles, and she collapsed on the bed and burst into tears.

Lilliputian tears were different from giant tears. Whenever Gulliver cried, whole buckets poured from his cheeks and soaked the floor with splashes. Lilliputian tears were much smaller. They hung in the air around her head, like mist.

"You're Lily, aren't you?" the boy whispered.

She looked up. Through her tears he was hazy. Why was he asking that? He was supposed to be squashing her, or slicing her up, or selling her to a circus.

"Why are you crying?" he said.

"Because of you, you horrible yahoo!" Lily sobbed. "I don't want to be stamped on, and I don't want to be sold to a circus, and I don't want to be eaten! I just want to go home! Why won't you giants let me go home?"

She looked down at the boy for an answer.

And he lay there, trying to find one.

"I thought you were a mouse," he said eventually.

Lily stopped crying at once and scowled. "A mouse!" She waved away her tears. "I'm not a mouse."

The boy shook all over. It was as if his brain did not believe his eyes and was trying to fling them out of his

76

head. He picked himself up out of the pond of porridge. "I see that now. You look more like a fairy."

"Furry!" cried Lily. "First you call me a mouse, and now you call me furry—"

"Not 'furry,' a fairy," said the boy quickly. "You know, a sprite. Or a goblin."

"Goblin!" yelled Lily. Now she was really furious.

"Maybe you're just little," he said hastily.

"I'm not little," Lily sniffed. "*You're* big." Suddenly she stopped and squinted up at him. "Why aren't you eating me?"

The boy reared back. "Eat you? Don't be disgusting!"

"Why?" said Lily, offended. "What's wrong with me? I'm probably delicious. Are you going to chop me up into little bits first, is that it? So you can feed me to your friend?"

"Chop you up? Feed you to my friend?" The boy looked helplessly confused. He blinked. "I don't have any friends," he added quietly.

"What about the one that tried to eat Squeak?" Lily demanded.

"You mean Horatio?" The boy flushed red. "Horatio isn't my friend, Lily. He's Mr. Plinker's cat."

Lily stepped back as the realization hit her. "Oh," she said, thinking back to what the boy had said. "*Ohhhh.*"

"He's Mr. Plinker's mouse catcher," the boy said. "And I'm Mr. Plinker's clock winder. His apprentice."

Lily felt herself blushing. So this boy wasn't cruel, after all. He had saved Squeak. Was he here to save her too?

The boy kneeled on the floor to sit with his face inches away from her.

"The whole city thinks Gulliver is crazy," he whispered. "I thought so too. Sometimes, when I was winding up the clocks, I heard him up here, talking to himself." The boy looked at Lily, and he was smiling. "But he's not crazy, is he? He was talking to *you*. Lily from Lilliput. When I read your note I could barely believe it. But now I know—it's all true."

His eyes were close now, very close. They were blue as skies and full of wonder.

Lily gasped.

For the first time, she could see. Not just into his eyes, but *past* them. To the place where all his thoughts flew around like birds.

It was incredible.

It was marvelous.

It was *magic*.

"Don't blink!" she cried at him. "Come closer! Let me see!"

"See what?" said the boy, blinking. His hands flew up to touch his face. "Did I get porridge on my nose?"

"*Shhh,*" she hissed, gazing through his eyes and into him.

Lily stared at hundreds and hundreds of giant thoughts. They were flying, swirling. Whole flocks of them. Gulliver's head had been a map she hadn't known how to read. All his thoughts were hidden like buried treasure. But this boy was different. When Lily looked inside him she saw a story—his story—and she read it in his eyes as if they were pages of a book.

She saw herself, the birdcage, Gulliver. She saw a trapped bird in a cruel clock, a jagged watch coiled on a slender wrist...

She saw the boy's name.

It was Finn. Finn Safekeeping. All of Lily's worries about him fell away then, because she could see. Finn wasn't here to hurt her, or snatch her, or bleed her dry with leeches.

He had come to set her free.

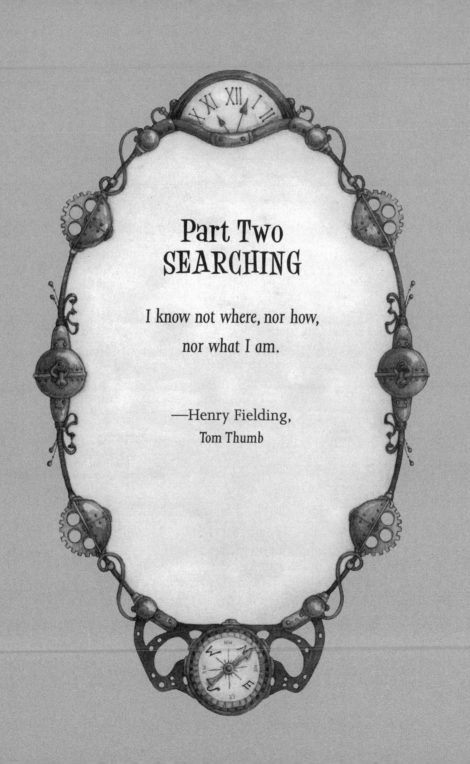

Part Two
SEARCHING

I know not where, nor how,
nor what I am.

—Henry Fielding,
Tom Thumb

14

Lily & Finn

They both had questions. Lily could feel them crowding around her head, waiting for her to blurt them out.

"Why are you saving me?" she wanted to yell. "Where are we going? When can you take me home?"

But Lily couldn't ask Finn, because there wasn't time for answers. Not with Gulliver snoring on the floorboards. They had to get away. Fast.

"Finn Safekeeping!" she cried. "What are you waiting for?"

His jaw dropped. "How do you know my—?"

"I can see it in your eyes," Lily interrupted. "And I know you're here to rescue me, so hurry up and do it!"

Bouncing off the bed, she landed on his palm. Finn lifted her up and the air around her went *whoosh!*—it felt like flying. She laughed. Never in her wildest escape plans did she ever think that a giant would get her out of the attic.

Somehow, though, it made sense. It felt right. They were together. From now on it was Lily and Finn. Finn and Lily. Their journeys had woven into one.

"Here." Finn plonked her down on his shoulder. "Hold tight!"

"Don't be a dimwit!" she yelled into his ear. "I've got to sit somewhere secret."

She tobogganed down his arm, leaped from his wrist, and vanished into his waistcoat pocket. "I'll stay hidden in here," she said, popping her head out. "Nice and snug. Now go!"

It felt like being catapulted through the air. Across the landing and down the stairs they flew, leaving Gulliver alone in his room with his cold porridge, his half-burned book, and his empty birdcage.

Lily gasped at the speed. Gulliver might have taken her far, far away from Lilliput, but Finn ran faster than the wind. He flew down the stairs, his feet barely touching the ground. It was incredible. Exhilarating. It made her giddy with hope.

Lily's mind soared with possibilities. At this speed, home didn't seem so out of reach. Finn could whisk her back to Lilliput in no time at all. He could leap over mountains and splash through oceans as if they were puddles.

It's possible, she told herself. *Anywhere and anything is possible, when you're in a giant's pocket.*

By sundown she could be running up the beach toward Nana and the village. It would be just like she'd imagined. The big'uns would light a fire and the little'uns would sit around it and listen as she told them her adventures.

Nana would cook pincher-crab pies, and play her *stringalin,* and they'd all sing songs and dance by the flames. They would light dandelion seeds in the embers and let the wind whisk them up into the night like floating lanterns, to light the way for the angels...

"We're here," Finn whispered, slowing to a stop.

"Where?" said Lily breathlessly.

"Let me show you." Finn reached his hand inside the pocket and brought Lily out.

15

Wound-Down Clocks & a Waste-Not Watch

L ily had to hide her disappointment. Of course they weren't home—they were in the middle of Mr. Plinker's workshop. In the light of day she saw the room clearly for the first time.

It was as damp as a swamp, as filthy as a gutter, as smelly as an armpit. Just behind Finn was the counter where Lily had saved Mr. Plinker's life. The Astronomical Budgerigar still sat there, but the clock maker was nowhere to be seen. His blood had left a dark stain on the wood.

In front of Lily was a huge bow-fronted window with panes of foggy glass, and a door with a little brass bell on it that rang whenever a customer entered. A spongy rug sat beside an unlit fireplace. Nailed to each of the four walls were hundreds upon hundreds of clocks.

Not one of them ticked. They were all quiet. Still. Their faces hung on the wall like portraits in a gallery.

"I woke up at sunrise and unwound them all," Finn murmured. "Every clock in the workshop. I even snuck up to Mr. Plinker's bedroom, too, and unwound his alarm clock."

So there are four levels to the shop, Lily thought, all stacked on top of each other: the attic, Mr. Plinker's bedroom, the workshop, and the basement.

"He won't wake up now," Finn said. "Listen." He pointed up at the ceiling and, through the boards, Lily heard the greasy gurgle of the clock maker's snores.

"Yuck," she said. "Sounds like he's blarting out of his mouth. Smells like it too."

Finn stifled a laugh. "Even if he had a bath he'd still be cruel. He's evil, Lily. He's the most horrible man I've ever met. You must have seen on the night you came here what he did to that bird in the Astronomical Budgerigar."

Lily shivered and nodded.

"The poor thing is still in there," said Finn. "Can you hear?"

Lily listened, and over on the counter she heard the faint cry of a trapped bird.

"Skee...skee..."

"I wish I could free him, like I'm freeing you," said Finn sadly. "But it's too hard. He's tied to the perch,

86

inside the clock. I'd have to reach into the Astronomical Budgerigar to get him...and you saw what happened last time someone put their hand in that clock."

Lily shuddered, picturing Mr. Plinker's mangled hand.

"He's the worst clock maker in all of London, isn't he?" She remembered how she had described Mr. Plinker when telling her story.

Finn's eyes grew wide, and he shook his head. "Oh, no, Lily. Not at all. Mr. Plinker is a genius—his clocks are masterpieces."

Lily frowned. "No, they're not. I always heard them from the attic. They never told the right time."

"That's because his clocks weren't invented to tell the right time." Finn paused and his eyes flicked up to the stairs, but Mr. Plinker snored on.

"Think about it," he said quickly. "Some people want clocks that run slow or fast on purpose. Before I came to work for Mr. Plinker I lived in an orphanage called the House of Safekeeping. That's where I got my last name. It was a horrible place. The beds and bread were both as hard as bricks. But the worst thing was the work.

"To keep the orphanage open, we had to sew shrouds and pillowcases. Then the owner of the orphanage, Mother Mary Bruise, sold them to the army.

"Mother Bruise went to Mr. Plinker and asked for a clock that would run fast when we ate our dinner, and slow when we sewed. That way Mother Bruise always had us working for longer. Mr. Plinker's clock made her rich."

Lily gasped. "That awful, Finn!" she cried. "That's monstrous! But what about all the angry customers? The ones I've heard bringing clocks back that have exploded?"

Finn shrugged. "Mr. Plinker often designs them to explode. Dukes and earls give his exploding clocks as gifts to their enemies."

Lily shook her head in disgust. So she had been wrong about Mr. Plinker—not only was he smarter than she'd thought, he was even nastier too.

"I wish I'd never stitched him back together," Lily fumed. "Still, Finn, at least you won't have to help him any more. When we get to Lilliput you can live with Nana and me, if you want." She looked at the front door, and grinned. "Come on, let's go!"

But to her surprise, Finn lowered her down to the floorboards and gently lifted her from his palm.

"I can't," he said softly, taking a step backward. "I've taken you as far as I can, Lily. You'll have to find your own way home."

"But...but, why?" Lily spluttered. She ran toward him, but Finn shuffled back again and looked away.

"Finn, do you *like* being Mr. Plinker's apprentice?"

Finn shook his head. "I hate it," he said bitterly. "I always have."

"Then let's run away!" Lily blurted. She almost laughed, it was so obvious. "Together! You have to come, Finn. I've seen London. I know how big it is. I won't survive if I go out there on my own."

Finn shut his eyes, and his hand went to rub his wrist, where his watch ticked. "Neither will I," he said.

Lily didn't understand. She didn't know what to say. Finn was meant to come with her. She knew it. The two of them were connected. They were both trapped, they both wanted to be free, and so they should both escape. Together. Lily and Finn. Finn and Lily.

"Why won't you come?" she said. "I need you, Finn Safekeeping. To keep me safe. To be my safekeeper."

Finn bit his lip. "Here." He reached into his pocket and held out something in his enormous fingers: a shiny sliver of silver as long as her arm. "Take this. I can't keep you safe, but this might."

Lily stared numbly at the giant needle. Then she grabbed it and tossed it angrily away. "What's wrong?" she demanded. "Why won't you tell me?"

"Because it won't make any difference," Finn said sadly. "Just go, Lily. Time's ticking, and you don't have time."

As he spoke, Finn's watch went ding-dong, and Lily saw it coil tighter on his wrist, like a snake tightens around its prey. Finn clenched his teeth to stop himself crying out. Hugging his arm to his chest, he shut his eyes against the pain.

"Finn?" Lily said in horror. "Finn, loosen that strap if it's too tight."

He looked up, buckets of tears in his big blue eyes. "I can't." His voice was strained. "Only Mr. Plinker can unwind the Waste-Not Watch."

"The What-Not Whatsit? What's that? Finn?" Lily ran forward and kicked his toe to get his attention. "I'm not going anywhere until you tell me!"

Finn slumped backward onto the stairs. For a long moment he sat with his jaw clenched and his eyes shut. Then he let loose a weary sigh that nearly blew Lily over. "All right then," he said. "I'll tell you. I'm Mr. Plinker's prisoner."

Lily saw in his eyes that it was true. But even as she heard the words she didn't understand them. How could Finn be a prisoner when he wasn't in a prison?

"This is my cage," Finn said, raising his arm. The sunbeams caught the watch on his wrist.

It was then that Lily learned something she would never again forget. She learned that the world was full of cages, and not all were built of iron. Some were made of lies or promises or secrets or questions.

Finn's cage was made of time. It had no walls, no locks, and no guards. But it was inescapable.

It was called the Waste-Not Watch.

16

Freedom & Fur

The Waste-Not Watch was the greatest of Mr. Plinker's inventions—and the cruelest. It worked in a way quite unlike any other clock in the entire world.

Most clocks are made to keep track of the time. The vast majority measure minutes and hours, mornings and afternoons. But the Waste-Not Watch measured something else.

It measured something similar, and yet something entirely different.

Something that was Finn's, and Finn's alone.

The Waste-Not Watch measured his lost time. Time he wasted. Seconds spent daydreaming, playing. Hours spent laughing, living...

The clock tallied up all this time—time that could be spent working on Mr. Plinker's clocks—and the more the Waste-Not Watch ticked, the tighter it wound on Finn's wrist.

An hour of wasted time made his fingers tingle.

Wasting two hours turned them blue.

Finn would not dare to waste three hours. If he did, the Waste-Not Watch would tighten right down to his bone, and his hand would shrivel and fall from his arm like a dead leaf.

"At the end of each day I shall unwind your wasted minutes," Mr. Plinker had told Finn, showing him the copper key on a chain around his neck. "But only if you work like a slave for me, boy. Only if you do *everything* I say—unless you'd rather be a one-handed beggar, starving on the street."

Finn had wanted to scream. He had wanted to cry. But screaming and crying wouldn't do him any good, because he would always be trapped. Like the bird in the Astronomical Budgerigar, he was a prisoner of Mr. Plinker's cruel imagination.

There was no one to set him free.

"Oh yes there is!" Lily answered when she saw the thought in his eyes. "There is someone who can free you, Finn—me!"

Lily scurried up Finn's leg and jumped from his knee onto his wrist. Before he could stop her, she stuck her hand inside the watch.

"Lily!" Finn hissed. "What are you doing?"

"Rescuing you, just like you rescued me!" Lily answered. Her whole arm rooted inside the machine, fingers brushing past sharp-toothed cogs.

"Take your hand out, Lily," Finn pleaded. "Take it out, while you still can!"

Lily gulped and wiped the sweat from her brow with her free arm. The clock ticked and buzzed in her ear as she reached farther in. She knew Finn was right. If she poked or prodded in the wrong place, the Waste-Not Watch could bite off her hand.

"There's a reason we found each other," she told him. "We're the keys that unlock each other's cages."

It was hard to explain how she knew this. It was more a feeling than a thought. Lily needed Finn, and he needed her.

"But—"

"Finn Safekeeping!" said Lily fiercely. "Trust me! And keep still!"

Finn stared openmouthed. "I will," he said at last. "I do trust you, Lily. Even though we've only just met. I really do."

Lily looked up at him. Into his eyes. She could see that he meant it.

And that felt wonderful.

Then doubt flickered into his gaze. "But how? You don't know anything about clocks, do you?"

Lily scowled and said nothing. She just kept poking and prodding the insides of the watch until she found what she was looking for.

"They should be around here somewhere... Where are they?"

"Where are the what?" asked Finn anxiously.

Suddenly her face lit up. "There you are!" she cried, and then her face darkened again. "Poor things...you're trapped. All caged up somehow."

"What are they?" Finn was wide-eyed.

"Wasted seconds," said Lily. "Oh, hundreds of them, all imprisoned inside. It's full to bursting with them. They're what's squeezing you so bad."

Finn gaped in amazement.

Lily frowned as she felt around the wasted seconds. They were packed in the clock so tight, and they couldn't get out. How was the Waste-Not Watch doing it? Magic? Mechanics? Alchemy?

Whatever it was, Finn was right—Mr. Plinker was a genius.

"Giants love keeping things in cages," said Lily darkly. She turned her attention back to the wasted seconds. "Poor things," she murmured to them. "All trapped. All squashed. I'll free you."

"Yes," Finn whispered, clenching his jaw. "Yes, Lily. Free them. Hurry."

She took a deep breath. "My hand's around a cog right now... And if I twist it this way..."

The buckle tightened on Finn's arm and he cried out. The hand of the Waste-Not Watch had just added another ten minutes to the total of his wasted time.

"Sorry!" said Lily. "I'll turn it the other way."

"No, don't!" Finn cried.

But Lily, with a heave, pulled at some part of the mechanism and—miraculously—let loose the wasted seconds. She couldn't see them, but she felt them go. They all flew free in one long moment that seemed to stretch out and last for ages.

At last, the buckle loosened. The hand of the Waste-Not Watch spun counterclockwise in a whirl, and Lily jerked her hand free, shouting, "Do it! Take it off!"

Finn pushed the strap and it slid from his wrist. The Waste-Not Watch went over his hand, fell to the floor, and cracked like an egg on the rug. Black oil spilled out of it, and a purple spark flew into the air like a firework.

"You did it," Finn said, stunned. "You freed me."

"It was easy," Lily blushed. "I'm good at getting out of cages."

Finn grinned, rubbing his poor swollen wrist. Lily saw his hand throbbing in pain. But at least it was still attached to his body.

"Oh, Lily." He smiled and blinked, and a tear fell down his cheek. "Thank you."

"Hey!" Lily yelled as the tear splashed right by her feet. "Why are you blubbering buckets? Now we can go! We can get out of here—together!"

Finn grinned and leaped over to the counter. He frantically plonked things into his waistcoat pocket—a little brown penny, a thimble, Lily's scrap of paper, an iron key...

"Hey!" cried Lily, running over the rug toward him. "What's going on?"

Finn paused with a hunk of bread in his fist. "I'm packing!" he said, face flushed with excitement. "We're getting away from Mr. Plinker for good."

Lily caught a few crumbs as they dribbled down from the bread and gobbled them up. She was ravenous.

"Well, remember to pack me too, you *mungle boff*," she mumbled with her mouth full of bread.

97

"I will," Finn grinned. "I'm done. Let's go!"

Shaking her head, Lily scurried across the workshop toward him. A moment later, Horatio padded softly down the stairs with a rat hanging limp in his jaws.

17

Plinker & Horatio

The cat was so close that Lily could have reached out and stroked him. The sound of his ginger fur swished in her ears like long grass in a summer breeze. Lily froze, but Horatio walked straight past her.

He plopped his prize on the rug—*splat*. Then he dipped his head and, with a rumbling purr, started to suck the stringy guts from the rat like Lilliputian *squighetti*.

"Shoo!" Finn hissed, too far away to scoop Lily to safety. "Shoo, Horatio!"

It was the wrong thing to say. Horatio looked up from his dinner, tail flicking, back arched. Lily saw herself reflected in the creature's huge green eyes.

Before Finn could move Horatio crouched and pounced. He flew through the air, swiping with his claws.

Lily screamed and tried to jump back, but she slipped on the oil from the Waste-Not Watch and fell.

Ginger fur whooshed over her in a blur.

Finn lunged for the cat, but Horatio hissed and in one fluid motion he turned and jumped away again. Lily barely had a chance to stand up straight before his claws raked through the air, an inch from her face. She fell back again, and her fingers found something.

Finn's needle.

"I'm not your breakfast!" Lily screamed, and she held out the needle with her two hands.

Horatio had already jumped. He couldn't stop. The silver point went straight into the soft, fleshy part of his paw.

With a deafening screech Horatio recoiled, licking his poor foot. A bright bead of blood rolled and then hung suspended on the white tip of a claw.

Finn reached over to snatch Lily to safety.

"That was for Squeak's tail!" she called from Finn's hand, shaking the needle at Horatio. "Go on, you horrible thing, shoo!"

Horatio gave a last hiss, then he scooped up the rat in his jaws and limped away toward the stairs.

"Are you hurt?" asked Finn breathlessly. "I thought you were—"

"I'm fine, you daft old *quog*!" Lily told him. She jumped in his pocket quickly, so he wouldn't see her shaking. Adrenaline was racing through her veins like lightning. "Just don't leave me lying around again! I'm delicate, you know."

Finn blushed and grinned with relief, but only for a moment.

The ceiling creaked, and a trickle of dust fell into the sunbeams. Somewhere above, a door slammed. And footsteps started on the stairs.

All the noise had woken Mr. Plinker.

A smell came oozing down the stairway. A smell of rot and swamps.

"Oh, no," Finn whispered. His hand plunged into his pocket and began to pull out handfuls of the things he had packed. Lily's note dropped to the floor, then a button and the hunk of bread.

"Unwind my alarm clock, did you, boy?" Mr. Plinker's voice was deep and wet. It poured into Lily's ears like oil.

She hid in the pocket, terrified. Why wasn't Finn running?

Then she understood—the iron key in his pocket unlocked the front door.

"It's here!" she hissed, pulling his fingertips in the right direction. "No, not there! *Here!*"

"Running away, Finn?" A laugh bubbled up from

Mr. Plinker's lips, like squelch from a swamp. "Have you forgotten about my Waste-Not Watch, boy? You can't escape. Besides, where will you go? No one in this city cares for you. Only me."

For a moment Finn faltered. Then he found his voice and his fingers found the key. "That's not true any more," he said. "Someone does care. I'm not your prisoner now."

Mr. Plinker choked on his chuckles as he spotted the ruins of his Waste-Not Watch on the floor. "You despicable boy! What have you done? That was my greatest invention, and you smashed it!"

Finn looked at Lily in his pocket. "You might want to cover your ears now," he whispered to her, slipping the key in the door. "And hold your nose."

"Where did you get that key?" Mr. Plinker hissed. Suddenly he was rushing down the stairs. "What's that in your pocket? Boy! *Answer me!*"

But Finn twisted the key in the lock, threw open the door, and ran out into the light. The clock maker's shouts were swallowed up by the city of giants.

18

Reek & Clamor

Up in Lily's birdcage the city had been a faraway rumble—something distant, like the waves at low tide. Down here in the streets it was deafening. She covered her ears and gasped.

Then the smell hit her too and she almost fainted. It lay over the street like a blanket. And just as a blanket is woven from a thousand smaller threads, so the stink of London was made up of a million interweaving stenches, reeks, and stinks, all intertwined together.

Horse muck mingled with the lavender of perfume shops. Soot and smoke blended with roasting coffee. Fresh bread baked, turnip tops rotted, tar bubbled, and beef broth boiled.

London was a city of reek and clamor.

But there was something else besides. It landed on Lily's cheek like a kiss, wonderful and warm.

It was the sun, glinting through the weave of the pocket. Lily raised up a hand until her fingertips were outside in the air. It was very good to be in Finn's waistcoat, safe, with the warm light soaking her skin. An entire moon she had been in that attic and the only sunbeams she ever got were weak ones, peeking through the window at the day's end.

"Yuck!" she said suddenly. "What's that smell?"

Finn darted into an alleyway to catch his breath. "The city," he panted. "The sewers. The river. You'll get used to it."

She shook her head. "Not that. Something else. It's worse. It smells like a thousand *slubbers* all sitting in their own *oik*."

Finn took a few deep sniffs and shook his head. "I can't smell anything."

"Lucky you," grumbled Lily. "It stinks. And it's getting closer."

Suddenly she realized—it wasn't a thousand *slubbers* sitting in their own *oik* at all.

"It's Mr. Plinker!" she yelled. "He's chasing us! Run, Finn!"

Finn whirled around. "Where?" he said in a panic. "I can't see him!"

Lily stuck her head from the pocket and followed her nose, trying to find the clock maker.

"Go left!" she cried as Mr. Plinker came rushing in from the right.

"Running away with Gulliver's secret, are you?" he bellowed, and in his fingers was a tiny scrap of paper.

It was Lily's note.

"I always knew he had something up there," Mr. Plinker shouted down the alley. "I didn't know he had *someone.*"

The clock maker lunged forward, but Lily's nose had given Finn a head start. He skidded around the corner as Mr. Plinker grabbed at empty air. Lily rattled around the pocket with Finn's remaining things—the penny, thimble, and needle—as they pelted down the street and plunged into a crowded market.

Suddenly there were giants everywhere, more giants than Lily thought could exist. They chit-chatted, chin-wagged, and haggled. She gasped and covered her ears. There were so many, and they were so loud! How did the land not sink into the sea under all their weight? How did the sky not shatter from all their noise?

The giants stomped past, and Lily peeked out at them. They carried whole fields of food on trays: walnuts like boulders, huge forests of carrots, leeks, and spinach.

A butcher carried a bucket of grease and gray meat crusted with old blood. A woman with a boiled-red face

came up to him and bought a hog's head the size of a house.

"Get yer offal!" he bellowed at Finn, shaking his tray. There was a sound inside like a hundred wet mops slopping over dirty floors. "Chitterlings! Tripe! Giblets!"

"Can you smell him?" Finn murmured at Lily. "I think we've lost him. I think we've—"

"Lost me, have you, boy?"

Mr. Plinker! He was there. In the crowd.

"He's got me, Lily!" Finn cried, trying to wrestle free. "Get away! Go!"

"Too late!" Mr. Plinker smirked, and his fingers slithered in the waistcoat pocket like eels.

Lily gritted her teeth. If she couldn't escape, she would have to fight. Just as Mr. Plinker's fingers wriggled around her foot, she gripped the needle like a sword.

Whoosh! The pocket vanished as Mr. Plinker whipped her into the air. Lily dangled upside down in front of his eyes. For a moment she gazed into them. They were dark as caves. The black thoughts squirming and slithering in them made her want to scream.

"What's this I've got a hold of?" he whispered.

"It's a foot," Lily said. "And it already belongs to me!"

Raising the needle, she jabbed Mr. Plinker's thumb as hard as she could.

He threw her into the air with a scream. Up Lily went, the needle flashing in the sun beside her. For a moment, she hung there alongside it, suspended, as if the Ender's invisible hand had stitched her onto the sky. Then she was tumbling down, head over heels, stomach plunging...

Lily shook her dizzy head. She lay in a hamper of sheep's wool, carried by a wrinkly giant lady like a basket of clouds. Climbing up the swaying wicker sides, Lily jumped again.

She landed on a wheelbarrow of apples, slipped, slid down the back of a blue swishing cloak, and then rolled into the gutter. The mud went *splash*. It was deep. It sucked her in.

"Help!" she called, up to her waist already, not caring who heard. "Help me!"

All around her, feet stomped and crashed. No one saw. She looked around in panic for a way to pull herself out. It was too late. The mud was up to her armpits.

As she flailed around, her fingers gripped something. Lily pulled it out from the sludge. A hollow straw of hay, as long as she was tall. Lily put one end to her lips, and pointed the other end upwards. As long as it stayed clear of the mud she could breathe through it and stay alive. The mud seeped up to her neck.

At last she could no longer struggle. She gathered all the breath she had for one last scream, then bit down on the hay stalk.

Let Finn find me, she prayed to the Ender.

There nothing to do but let the mud take her. She focused on the straw. On each precious sip of air. Sludge bubbled up her nose. Her eyes oozed below the surface. The mud swallowed Lily whole.

19

Lost & Found

Lily was stuck at the bottom of a bowl of Gulliver's porridge. She was eating her way to the top before she drowned, but after a few mouthfuls she had to stop, because the porridge was full of tiny pebbles and tasted like dirt.

In fact, it *was* dirt.

Suddenly she woke from the dream and remembered: Mr. Plinker, the gutter, the straw...

Lily sat up with a start, spitting out earth and gulping air. Mud was everywhere—she had to scoop it from her ears, blink it from her eyes, sneeze it from her nose. She squinted through the grit, trying to see where she was. Then the world turned sideways and she plunged into cold water.

She flailed around until her feet found a floor and her fingers found a rim. Lily pulled herself up to the surface, the mud sliding off in slabs. At last she could see, and she knew she was safe.

She'd tumbled into a teacup, and holding it was…

"Finn!" she spluttered. "You look awful."

He managed a smile. "I suppose I do," he said. Muck was splattered over his clothes and sweat dribbled clean streaks down his grimy face. He looked exhausted.

"You found me," she said. "*Again*. I knew you would."

"I always will," he promised. "And look what else I found."

"M-my needle!" Lily shivered, reach-ing out her hand for it and swishing it back and forth. "This little sliver saved m-m-my life—twice! I think I'll c-call it Stabber."

"That's a good name," Finn nodded. "Now come and get dry before you freeze."

Lily tucked Stabber under her arm. Then she climbed out of the teacup and Finn threw it back onto the trash pile where he had found

it. Lily toweled her hair dry on his sleeve, but her teeth wouldn't stop chattering.

"M-m-m-my d-d-dress is r-r-ruined," she said. The silk was still caked with mud.

"You just get warm," said Finn. He cupped his hands together and she climbed into his palms, shivering and coughing.

"I feel like a bird in a nest," she said. It was dark now. How long had she been sunk in the mud? Hours and hours. So long, she'd fallen asleep.

"Where are we?" She gazed around. Sheer brick walls rose on either side, almost up to the stars.

"Just an alleyway," Finn said. "After you jabbed Mr. Plinker with Stabber I managed to get away from him and hide here."

At the mention of the clock maker, Lily's shivers got worse. "Is he gone?" she whispered.

Finn nodded. "Thanks to you," he said with a grin. "He took one look at the needle you jabbed in his thumb, and fainted."

"It was only a pinprick," she said, wiping Stabber clean. "He can't have lost that much blood!"

Finn shook his head. "He didn't faint from loss of blood, Lily—he fainted because he was terrified. My master only cares about ten things in the whole world—

his fingers and thumbs. They're his tools. He can't make his clocks without them. You didn't know it but you hit Mr. Plinker right in his Achilles heel!"

Lily frowned. "His heel?"

"I meant his weak spot," said Finn. "It's a... Oh, never mind. All you need to know is, Mr. Plinker fainted. Headfirst into that butcher's bucket of giblets."

Lily laughed. Knowing that made her feel a tiny bit warmer.

"I saw you fall in that woman's wool basket," Finn continued. "Then you jumped and I lost sight of you. I searched the market from top to bottom, but you were gone."

Lily grimaced as she picked the mud from her dress. "How did you find me?"

"I searched. For hours and hours, until it was so cold I couldn't feel the end of my nose, and so dark that I could barely see beyond it, either. Then, just when I was at the end of my hope, I saw something. A little white puff of mist coming up from the gutter.

"I went nearer. I saw it again, coming out of a straw. It was your breath, Lily. Your breath, misting in the cold. I pulled you out and...here we are."

For a while the two of them sat in silence, gazing down the alleyway at the cobbles. At the moon. At the midnight slugs, laying their silver paths.

Here I am, Lily thought. *What now?*

She looked at Finn. The boy who had set her free, saved her life, and given her hope. They could go anywhere now. Do anything. Lily wasn't a prisoner any more.

So why did she still feel trapped?

Finn brought her up in his hands and frowned. "You look miserable," he said. "Is it the cold? The mud? The belly rumbles?"

She shook her head.

"What is it, then? Why do you look sad?"

"Because," she said. "You found me, but I still feel lost."

"You want to go home," he said quietly.

Lily nodded miserably. "I don't know where it is, though," she said. "I came across the sea from Lilliput, but I've been caged up for so long, I don't know where I am. Or even who I am."

She sat in Finn's hands, finally understanding the truth. Escaping from Gulliver was just the beginning. Now she had to search. She had to find Lilliput. She had to find her place in the world.

Lily gazed up at her friend. "When you came for me, I thought getting home would be easy. You ran so fast I thought I'd be home by sundown." She looked at the moon and covered her face with her hands. "But that's nonsense, isn't it? It's blumbercrock. I've spent half of my life in pockets and cages and socks. I didn't realize how big the world is. How can I search something so enormous?"

Finn thought for a long time. "I'll help you," he said eventually. "We'll search together."

"But it's impossible," she whispered bitterly. "It took you all day just to find me in this market, didn't it? Finding Lilliput will take a thousand lifetimes!"

Finn shook his head. "You can't think like that." He sounded fierce. "You can't, Lily. You have to hope. Hope is how I found you in the mud."

"It wasn't," she said. "You saw my little puff of breath—"

"But what about the hours and hours before that? If my hope had run out then, I never would have found you. Don't you see?"

Lily did see. Maybe Finn was right. This city was just a freckle on the face of the earth. Which meant Lily was just a smidgen on a speck on a fleck of a freckle. But if she gave up hope, she would be nothing at all.

"I'll try," she muttered. "But it's hard when the world is so big, and you don't even know where to start."

"I know where to start." Out of nowhere a crafty smile crept across Finn's face, like a fox over a field. "We start by warming our toes and filling our bellies."

Lily's stomach gurgled like an empty drain. "You're right," she admitted grudgingly. "We'll never find Lilliput on an empty stomach!"

Finn's smile grew even wider. He took the little brown penny from his pocket. "I know just who we need to see. Someone who will warm us up and fill us to the brim..."

As he got to his feet, Lily saw two names in his eyes.

"Who's Mr. Ozinda?" she asked. "And what on earth is hot chocolate?"

20

Mr. Ozinda & His Chocolate House

"Mr. Ozinda will cheer us up. Hot chocolate is just what we need." That's all Finn would say. He scooped up Lily and sped out of the alley. It was late. No one walked the midnight streets but a sorry-looking chimney sweep who left black footprints behind him.

There was little for Lily to do while Finn walked, so she busied herself by widening a small hole near the bottom of the pocket. After a few pokes with Stabber it was big enough for her to peek through without being seen.

She gazed at the candlelit windows flickering past, wondering where she and Finn were headed. Who was Mr. Ozinda? His name didn't sound like any other giant she had met. Perhaps, like Lily, he came from somewhere else.

She tried asking Finn questions, but apart from finding out that Mr. Ozinda was a Spaniard (whatever that was), she only heard Finn mumbling about street names and left turns and roads they had to cross to reach their mysterious destination.

He ran into a square where the houses were stacked very neatly, side by side, like books on a shelf. Tucked away, just around the corner, was a two-story building. Lily looked at the elegant sash windows and the great golden O swinging on a sign above the doors.

"There it is," Finn said, licking his lips. "There's Mr. Ozinda's Chocolate House."

As Lily watched the doors, they opened. Out onto the street squeezed the biggest giant she had ever seen. His body was shaped like a pear, his skin was the color of syrup, and his name (of course) was...

"Mr. Ozinda!"

Finn waved and called his name again, and Mr. Ozinda answered back in his sing-song voice: "If your spirits be low and your body be thin, wipe your feet on the mat and come right in!"

Everything about Mr. Ozinda was gigantic—from his hearty appetite to his sparkling cheerfulness to his huge wobbly bottom.

Lily liked him at once.

"Mr. Ozinda," Finn began. "It's me—Finn...from the orphanage! From the House of Safekeeping!"

"Of course!" said Mr. Ozinda. "Finn! Finn! Where

have you been? Last Christmas I go like always to the orphanage and give out my hot chocolate. But you are not there. 'Where is Finn?' I say. And the orphans all tell me: 'Gone away with Mr. Plinker.'"

Finn nodded. "It's true. Mother Mary Bruise caught me tinkering with the clocks Mr. Plinker had sold her."

"Tinker and Plinker," Mr. Ozinda said with a silly grin. "But why ever did you do that?" he added, serious again.

"Whenever we orphans were working, Mr. Plinker had designed them to tick slowly. And whenever we were resting, they sped up. It was horrible."

"Yes!" said Mr. Ozinda. "Last Christmas Day at the orphanage was only forty minutes long. I went there first thing in the morning, and everyone was getting ready for bed!"

"It wasn't fair. So I waited until the dead of night. Then I crept up to the clocks and fixed them, but Mother Mary Bruise found out. I thought she was going to beat me, but instead she did something much worse. She took me straight to Mr. Plinker's workshop and sold me to him."

In the pocket, Lily's heart filled with pity.

Poor Finn, she thought. *Neither of us knows our parents, but at least I still have a home.*

"I became his apprentice," Finn continued. "No, that's not the right word. I became his slave. But not any more."

"No?" Mr. Ozinda raised his eyebrows. "That is good to hear. I cannot stand any man who smells worse than his pet. But let me ask...if you are not his apprentice, what are you now?"

Finn thought for a while. "I'm a safekeeper," he said simply, and in his pocket Lily smiled.

"A safekeeper?" Mr. Ozinda laughed and leaned closer. His voice sank to a murmur. "Well then, Mr. Safekeeping, what exactly are you keeping safe?"

Lily's smile vanished. *Finn, you mungle bof, you've said too much!* Mr. Ozinda looked curious, even hungry for an answer.

But Finn just shrugged and replied, "A secret told is a secret spread, I hide mine away in my pocket instead."

Mr. Ozinda laughed delightedly. It seemed Finn's rhyme had satisfied him. "Well said, Mr. Safekeeping the safekeeper, well said! Now you must enter, come, have a sniff!"

"A sniff?"

"A sniff of this wonderful whiff!" And Mr. Ozinda took the golden handles of his shop doors and threw them open. At once the smell—the rich, warm smell of chocolate—oozed out onto the street.

Lily closed her eyes, gulping down breath after breath of the heavenly aroma. Her nose feasted on the delicious air. If chocolate smelled like this, what would it *taste* like? Her mouth watered.

"Oh! I see—a whiff is not enough!" The Spaniard put his arm around Finn's shoulder and pulled him into the chocolate shop.

They moved past tables where portly giants sat flicking through newspapers and sipping daintily from cups. Candles lit everything with a soft, syrupy glow. Something swooped back and forth above Lily, finally landing on Finn's shoulder.

"*Buenos días,*" a voice rasped.

"Get away from my guest, you noisy pest!" Mr. Ozinda said with a chuckle. "Do not mind him, Finn. He is a good parrot."

Lily looked up at an enormous bird. At first his feathers appeared to be dull and colorless, but as he moved she saw they were actually a whole rainbow of grays—ash, slate, steel, cinereous, and silver. He was beautiful.

"You must be thinking: where did I get this wonderful pet?" said Mr. Ozinda fondly. "A present from Mrs. Ozinda, my wife. She travels the world, selling my chocolate treats to emperors, sultans, and kings, and she brings back all manner of marvelous things."

He motioned to some of the treasures adorning the walls. "Blankets embroidered with the histories of fallen empires. China pots as fragile as eggshells. But best of all, a talking bird who repeats back what he has heard. I have named him Señor Chitchat."

"*Hola*," called the parrot.

The Spaniard stroked him fondly. "Señor Chitchat speaks English, French, and Spanish. I am sure he can also speak Pigeon, Sparrow, and Swift. What a gift he has for languages!"

Mr. Ozinda led Finn to a gleaming brass counter, where cutlery and china cups lay immaculately arranged and the smell of cocoa was strongest. Señor Chitchat hopped onto his perch below the shelves, which were stacked with mountains of food.

There were pyramids of chocolate truffles, boxes of snuff tagged "Havana" and "Seville," and several bottles of drink. Through her hole Lily read the labels: cinnamon brandy, peach cider, and almond beer.

"Now," said Mr. Ozinda. "Sweet or creamy, good young sir? Which hot chocolate would you prefer?"

"Sweet *and* creamy, please," Finn ordered, dropping his coin into the Spaniard's palm.

"Ah! My daughter, Dumpling, likes her hot chocolate this way too. So! Two ounces of beans. Then add cream... three and a half spoons of sugar...stir with a little of what you English call...vigor! And, of course—it must be filled to the very brim!"

He wiped his hands on a towel, clicked his fingers together and said, with a theatrical flourish: "So! We begin!"

Lily watched as he scattered a handful of chocolate beans into a heavy mixing bowl, and then *bang! bang! bang!*—he pounded them to dust, using a huge boulder of marble.

He swept the powder onto a hot granite slab, then rolled it back and forth with an iron rolling pin. Very soon the chocolate began to melt into a gooey brown lake.

"Then this!" said Mr. Ozinda, adding pinch after pinch of spices from the seven jars to his left, throwing them all in one after the other. "Then this! Then this! Then this!"

He carried on until the liquid chocolate was dark, rich, and bubbling. It smelled delicious.

Mr. Ozinda took one of his tall teapots with a curved spout and, using a silver ladle, began to fill it with the chocolate mixture. He measured out the hot milk and cream, whirled them all together using a swizzle stick, then slid the pot over the counter toward Finn. He hadn't spilled a drop.

"*Voilà!*" squawked Señor Chitchat.

"Is done so neatly!" Mr. Ozinda announced. "And very sweetly! Enjoy!"

21

Rhyme & Slime

Finn took the teapot over to a bench in the corner, far away from the other customers. *Gloop-gloop-gloop* went the spout as he poured out a steaming cup of hot chocolate. Lily longed for just a drip. She bent down and scooped up the thimble that Finn kept in his pocket.

"Give us a slurp!" she whispered, holding it out.

Finn looked around anxiously at the portly gentlemen, but none of them paid him the slightest bit of interest. Most were dozing, with their wigs pulled down over their eyes. Mr. Ozinda was running his fat fingers around the rim of the chocolate bowl like a naughty child, and then looking around to see if anyone noticed.

"There!" Finn dipped her thimble in his cup. "That's a hundred slurps for you."

Lily gasped in delight. She took the steaming thimble in both hands and gulped down a mouthful.

It was like swallowing happiness. As the hot chocolate spread through her, the hunger went from Lily's belly, the cold went from her toes, and the ache went from her heart. She was full to the brim with sweetness.

"Wonderful lovely," she sighed, raising the thimble and gulping the rest.

"Now we're ready to start searching," Finn mumbled, head drooping down to his chest.

"Yes," Lily yawned. "Now we're ready to start..." She was very snug and warm.

The fire crackled and popped. Voices murmured and newspapers rustled. It was the easiest thing to lie back in Finn's pocket and close her eyes.

Lily drifted off into a dream. There were angels in it, somewhere high above. They whispered secrets. And tiptoed over the ceiling. And giggled at being up past their bedtime.

Not angels, Lily realized as she dozed. *Children. In the bedroom above the shop.*

Then, as she listened, the children started to sing.

It wasn't the tune that pulled Lily from her dream. It wasn't the singing that almost stopped her heart. It was the words.

Have you heard of the tale
That's short and tall?
There's an island in the world
Where everything is small!

Lily poked her head from the pocket. "Finn," she hissed. "Can you hear that?"

But Finn just mumbled under his breath, chin on his chest. He was asleep.

"I must still be dreaming," she whispered. But she wasn't. She was in Mr. Ozinda's chocolate shop, and the song carried on above her:

And the babies that are born there
Are tiny as peas,
And they wear little frocks
with itty-bitty sleeves...

"Finn!" Lily scrambled onto his lap, keeping under the table and out of sight of the other giants. "Wake up! They're singing about Lilliput!"

She poked him, prodded him, kicked his belly. Even jumped up and down on his fingers. Finn just smiled, as if he were being tickled.

What could she do? Climbing up his arm and bellowing in his ear would wake him, but what if someone saw?

She could always jab him with Stabber...but then Finn might jerk awake and catapult her into the fireplace.

"Finn!" Lily whispered. "You've got ten seconds to wake or I'm going up those stairs without you. Finn, are you listening?"

And they live in houses
no higher than your foot,
Have you heard about the island of
Lilliput?

It was impossible. Incredible. How did the children upstairs know about Lilliput? Lily's whole body quivered with excitement. She had to find out.

"I'm going, Finn. If you want to wake up, you better do it right now."

Finn mumbled something about a budgerigar.

That was it, then. Lily would go on her own. She had to. Maybe they were nothing but rhymes. But rhymes were often riddles too. And sometimes riddles led you in circles, but sometimes they led to an answer.

What if these rhymes led Lily home?

Keep to the shadows, she thought, looking at Mr. Ozinda's customers. *These giants aren't like Gulliver—they're old and sleepy, and they don't even know I exist. They're not looking for me, so they won't see me.*

Upstairs, the children started another song.

Show me a girl
the size of a spoon,
And a giant who can reach to the moon.

Lily could wait no longer. Sticking her finger in the thick hot chocolate, Lily splattered out two words on Finn's sleeve—*I'm upstairs.* Then she took Stabber, hooked it into her dress, and climbed down to the floor.

Show me an island
like a floating balloon,
And a horse that can sing this tune.

Darting from table leg to table leg, Lily edged around the counter as Mr. Ozinda popped cocoa beans into his mouth and chewed them slowly. She walked right under his feet—his belly and bottom were so big, he couldn't see the floor.

"*Hola,*" Señor Chitchat squawked at her from his perch.

"Silly thing," Mr. Ozinda sighed. "There is no one here!"

The door was open a crack. Lily squeezed through. The voices from the shop faded away and the singing grew louder. It was still just a whisper, though—even Lily's ears could barely hear it.

> Show me, Gulliver,
> And show me soon,
> Or I'll call you a liar and a loon!

Lily couldn't believe it. The children knew about Gulliver too!

She looked out across the room she now found herself in. It was dark and cold. A few slugs crawled over the stones. Lily passed piled-up sacks of cocoa beans, startling ants into cracks and wood lice into little balls, until suddenly she arrived at the foot of the stairs.

They loomed up into the darkness—each step an impossible climb. It would have been easy if Finn were there. Without him Lily would need the wings of a bird, or the legs of a spider...

Or the slime of a slug.

She sprinted back to them. Huge, gray, quivering things. They reminded her of Mr. Plinker's tongue. She shuddered. But there was no other way to climb those stairs.

Tugging up her sleeves, Lily rolled over one of the slugs and coated her hands and feet with slime. It glooped between her fingers and squelched between her toes.

"Sorry," she told the helpless creature. "I don't like this any more than you do."

Finally she rolled the slug back over and rushed to the stairs. The gunk was already beginning to stick, and her feet left sticky strands on the stone as she ran.

By the time she reached the staircase the slime was a thick glue. Lily rested her palm against the wooden step.

Please work, she thought. *Please stick.*

It did. The glue made climbing easy. Lily pulled herself up the sheer side, arm over arm, leg over leg, up and up. In no time at all she stood on the first step, looking at the second and the third and fourth and all the way to the top.

"Only another twelve to go," Lily said, hoping the slime would stick for that long.

She climbed onward, to the giggles and voices.

22

Hide & Seek

Someone had laid her on a rug. It was soft on her cheek. Lily blinked her eyes, trying to remember how she got there. She had been climbing up the stairs. Right to the top. Then, after the tenth step, something had happened...what?

Looking down at her hands, it came back to her. *The slug slime stopped sticking.* She groaned. Her head ached. How far had she fallen?

Far enough to knock myself out. I'm lucky I didn't break anything.

Slowly she sat up. Her head felt like a plate spinning on a stick, ready to wobble off her neck at any moment. She squeezed her eyes shut and waited.

After a while the swaying stopped. It was then Lily realized just how hard she had fallen. The dizziness was gone, but now she was hallucinating.

She had to be. Because what she saw was impossible.

She was in a bedroom, but it wasn't a giant's bedroom.

It was Lilliputian sized.

Lily looked around, amazed. For the first time in moons, she didn't feel tiny. There was a wardrobe she could open. Curtains she could close. A bed she could sleep in. Three armchairs for sitting...

But people sat there already. Watching her. Hidden in the gloom.

With a jump and a yell, Lily drew Stabber from her waist and pointed it at the shadowy figures.

"Who are you?" she asked, clutching her head as the giddiness started again. "Tell me!"

The figures did not answer, or even move.

"You're Lilliputians," Lily breathed. "What are you doing in London? Did you save me? I climbed up the stairs... I heard you singing... I thought you were giant children... I didn't realize you were Lilliputians!"

There was a long silence. Lily lowered the needle's point. "I'm sorry," she said, trying to clear her head. "I didn't mean to frighten you. I'm just...I fell and..."

Peering into the gloom she thought she saw the people smiling.

"Who are you?" she whispered, creeping forward step by step, needle in her hand. *"What* are you?"

The figures didn't answer. They kept staring at the rug. They were dolls, with glass eyes and cotton hair, their smiles painted on with a brush.

Lily stepped back, finally understanding. She sprinted to the window and stared out of the dollhouse.

A giant brown eye blinked back at her.

"I told you she was alive!" a voice gasped. "Told you, told you! Now we can play!"

There was an explosion of giggles and someone said, "Let us see, we can't see!"

The entire room trembled. Hinges screeched as the windowed wall swung outward like a door. Lily yelped, tripped over the rug and dropped Stabber.

A giant pudgy face peered in. "Hello, dolly," it whispered. "I'm Dumpling."

Dumpling's eyes were small and set a little too far apart. Her nose was an upturned snout. Her dark ringlets were bunched up with a ribbon, so that they looked like a pile of sausages. She wore a nightdress the color of butter.

"Shall we play princesses, little dolly? Shall we have a tea party?"

Lily didn't answer. She scooped Stabber from the rug and ran. Bursting through the door, she pelted down a dark hallway for the stairs. Outside, Dumpling clapped and giggled.

"Hide and seek! Hide and seek!" she sang.

Other voices whined: "Don't make her hide. *We* haven't seen her yet!"

The hallway filled with another face. A thin and watery-eyed girl with straw-colored hair and a glistening stream of slime running from her nostrils. This slug-nosed girl wore a nightdress as green as lettuce.

"Ooh," she cooed. "Pretty."

Lily barged into another bedroom, threw open a wardrobe, and dived in among the princess dresses and soldier outfits.

"Where are you, dolly?" Dumpling called.

"Come out, come out wherever you are!" said Slug-Nose.

"But I still haven't seen her!" a third voice whined.

"Then find her. Ready or not, dolly, here we come!"

Lily crouched in the wardrobe, listening to the giggling girls as they ransacked the dollhouse. They tossed aside beds and turned over bathtubs, hunting for her.

What a fool she'd been, leaving Finn! There were no clues here, just Mr. Ozinda's daughter having a sleepover.

But how could Dumpling and her friends know songs about Lilliput and Gulliver? And why didn't they realize that Lily was a Lilliputian—why did they call her a dolly?

Lily didn't know the full reason, but she knew part of it. The girls were stupid and selfish. And that made them dangerous.

Wake up, Finn, she prayed. *Wake up soon.*

Suddenly the wardrobe tipped forward and shook from side to side. Lily spilled out onto the floor along with a pile of dolly outfits. Staring down at her was a third girl sucking her thumb.

She doesn't look so bad, thought Lily.

"I found her!" said the girl, taking her thumb from her mouth.

Lily was almost sick. The thumb was a horrible sight. It had been stewing in the girl's mouth for so long that it was wrinkly and soft and bruised, like bad fruit.

Just the sight of it gave Lily the shivers. Plum-Thumb wore a purple nightdress with blue ribbons.

"We're having a sleepover, dolly," she said. "We were meant to be asleep hours ago, but Dumpling's papa has forgotten about us."

"Make her dance!" sang Slug-Nose in her thin, reedy voice. "Make her sing! Make her talk! Make her drink hot chocolate!"

"Hot chocolate," said Plum-Thumb, eyes glazing over with pleasure.

"It's my sleepover," said Dumpling. "And my dolly. I heard the noise on the stair. I went and found her. She'll do what I say. Won't you, dolly?"

"I'm not a dolly," said Lily.

The three girls shrieked and clapped.

"It talks!" they squealed. "The dolly talks!"

"You're much better than our other dollies," said Dumpling.

The girls nodded enthusiastically, grabbing their dolls from the armchairs in the room where Lily had awoken.

"This is Thumbelina," said Dumpling, holding up a redheaded dolly.

"This is Mrs. Ittle-Wittle," said Slug-Nose, holding up a doll with blonde hair.

"And this is Princess Henry," said Plum-Thumb. Princess Henry had black pigtails, tied with red ribbon.

"But they're just pretend," said Dumpling. "They're not special like you."

All at once the girls dropped their dollies and leaned forward, crowding around Lily.

"Magic talking dolly," said Slug-Nose. "We're going to have lots of fun together."

Plum-Thumb's eyes sparkled. "Play time," she said.

23

Trufferdunks & Tantrums

Grinning over Lily, the girls clapped and stared. Their mouths were all dirty brown teeth and spit, like unwashed plates in a sink. Lily saw right into their eyes, to all of their terrible thoughts. Slug-Nose was spiteful. Plum-Thumb was greedy. And Dumpling was used to getting her own way.

Lily was nothing to them but a toy to be played with.

And once they grew bored the girls would toss her aside.

She had to escape.

"I want to play princesses!" said Slug-Nose, wiping her oozing nose.

"I want to have a tea party, please!" said Plum-Thumb, elbowing her friend out of the way.

"I asked first," said Slug-Nose, barging her back.

"I said please," growled Plum-Thumb.

"Princesses!" said Slug-Nose.

"Tea party!" Plum-Thumb glared, giving her friend a pinch.

Slug-Nose yelped and pulled Plum-Thumb's hair. So Plum-Thumb stepped on Slug-Nose's foot "by accident," and Slug-Nose wiped snot down the back of Plum-Thumb's dress. She grinned and bent down to scoop up Lily, but then there was a horrible squirting sound as Plum-Thumb elbowed her in the nose.

Suddenly the two of them were kicking, punching, and biting each other, while hissing "Princesses!" and "Tea party!"

"Quiet!" Dumpling whispered, wrestling her fighting friends apart. "Stop being noisy or Papa will come!"

Lily looked up at the seething mass of arms, legs, and heads; a tangle of petticoats and pigtails. For now the girls had forgotten her—this was her chance to escape.

She opened the dollhouse door and crept across the floorboards. *Stomp, stomp, stomp* went the giant feet around her. Lily waited, saw her moment, and darted forward.

Something slammed into her side and she flew into the air and skidded on the floor. She lay there, doubled up, gasping for breath. Her chest felt broken.

"You kicked the dolly," said Dumpling. "Look."

The fight between the girls wound down, from punches to pinches to nasty looks, until they were all looking at Lily gasping weakly on the floor.

"You broke it," said Plum-Thumb to Slug-Nose. "It's dead."

"I didn't kick it," she sniffed back. "You did. Anyway, it's still alive. Look."

Lily sat up, sipping the air slowly back into her lungs. Her head and chest were aching, but worse than the pain was the fear.

The three girls didn't realize Lily was a person. To them she was just a toy—a toy they all wanted but couldn't all have. They were going to fight again and, sooner or later, Lily would get broken.

She had to escape. She had to wake Finn, or even bring Mr. Ozinda up here. But how? No one downstairs would hear her, no matter how loud she screamed for help. Suddenly an idea fell into Lily's head, like an egg into a pan, and started to sizzle away. A single, perfect, delicious idea. Perhaps she could use the girls' own stupidity against them. Despite the pain in her chest, Lily managed a smile.

"I'm not playing with any of you," she choked out, rubbing her sore ribs.

The girls were still arguing among themselves, and they didn't hear. So Lily stamped her feet and bellowed:

"I'M GOING TO TURN YOU ALL INTO TRUFFERDUNKS INSTEAD!"

The girls all stopped and looked down at her.

"What's a trufferdunk?" Slug-Nose asked.

"A trufferdunk," said Lily, thinking fast, "has the nose of an elephant, the eyes of a snail, the body of a toad, and the tail of a pig. It walks on its ears, eats with its feet, and burps out of its belly button. A trufferdunk is the most disgusting animal on all of the earth, and when I cast my spell, you're going to be turned into one! All three of you!"

Plum-Thumb and Slug-Nose shuffled back a little, but Dumpling stayed where she was. "You can't do spells," she sneered.

"I can," Lily lied. "Because I'm not a dolly at all. I'm a fairy."

The girls took another step back.

"A fairy?" Plum-Thumb squeaked.

"Don't listen," said Dumpling, whirling around. "She's tricking."

Lily grinned. "I'm not. I'm a fairy. What else can I be? I'm made out of stardust and blossoms and baby laughs. I'm as old as the hills and as wise as the owls. And unless you take me downstairs right now I'm going to turn all of you into trufferdunks for a hundred years!"

Dumpling snorted. "No such thing as a truffer-dunk," she said, but the others looked far from convinced.

"I don't want to burp out of my belly button," Slug-Nose whimpered.

"It's too late," Lily said, lowering her voice to a soft, deadly whisper. She drew Stabber from her dress as if it were a wand. "I can feel the fizzing in my fingers. I can feel the sparks in my eyes and the spell on my breath!"

She began to shake and swish Stabber around and around her head. Plum-Thumb let out a whimper of fear.

"*Hubblelunk, Bubbermunk, Flunnerstunk, Trufferdunk!*" Lily whispered, pretending to cast her spell. Then, louder: "*Hubblelunk, Bubbermunk, Flunnerstunk, Trufferdunk!*"

"Nooooo!" Slug-Nose wailed. "I'm sorry, fairy! I'm sorry!"

"Shh!" Dumpling hissed. "Papa will hear us!"

That was exactly what Lily hoped. She screwed her eyes shut. Summoning up every last bit of her strength, she bellowed: "HUBBLELUNK, BUBBERMUNK, FLUNNER-STUNK, TRUFFERDUNK!"

"Ahhhhh!" Plum-Thumb screamed. "Help! Help! The horrid fairy's making magic!"

Dumpling clapped her hands over her friend's mouth as if she could cram the words back in, but it was too late. Lily heard booming steps on the stairs, and a sing-song voice calling out, "Sweetheart, Pumpkin... my darling Dumpling! What is all this shouting for? You should be sleeping!"

Then another voice—one that filled Lily with relief—said: "I think I know, Mr. Ozinda."

"Finn!" Lily shouted, dropping Stabber to the ground and running to the door. "I'm in here!"

Slug-Nose, crouched on the floor with a pillow over her head, opened her eyes. "We're not trufferdunks!" she said happily.

Dumpling just glared at her friends and muttered under her breath. Then the door to her bedroom flew open and in squeezed Mr. Ozinda and Finn.

"Lily!" Finn cried. "Are you hurt?"

"Oh my," Mr. Ozinda breathed. "Oh my, oh me, oh what's this I see?"

24

Chit & Chat

Now it was dawn, and the stars were unstitching themselves from the blanket sky. Mr. Ozinda had emptied his shop of customers and sent Dumpling and her friends whining and stomping to bed. Lily could hear his stern voice as he scolded them in the bedroom above.

"Mumblemumblemumble...never tell...mumble-mumble...naughty girl...mumble...straight to hell..."

"Is it ready yet?" she asked, turning to Finn.

"*Reddy yeh? Reddy yeh?*" said Señor Chitchat on his perch above the counter, for Lily had said it so many times that the parrot had now started to copy her.

"Almost," Finn said again, dipping his finger into the porcelain egg cup he held over a candle flame. It was filled with soap suds and water.

"I only want it toasty," she reminded him. "Not scorchy."

He nodded. "I know. I think it's done."

Lily jumped up and down with excitement then winced at the pain. Her head and ribs ached more than ever. "Come on, then, let me get in!"

Carefully Finn put the egg cup into the bathroom of the dollhouse and swung the wall shut on its hinges. Mr. Ozinda had brought it down from Dumpling's room and placed it on a table by the fireplace.

"Yours," he had told Lily. "To stay in for as long as you wish."

Lily went in through the front door, threw off her dress, and sploshed into the soap suds and water.

"Wonderful lovely," she murmured, closing her eyes.

"Lily?" Finn called through the curtains.

She ducked down under the soap suds. "Get away from that window, Finn! I'm starkers in here!"

She almost heard the blood rushing to his face. "Oh! I just wanted to say don't be long. And don't fall asleep, either. Mr. Ozinda wants to speak to us when he comes back down."

She didn't answer. Whatever the Spaniard had to say, it wasn't more important than this bath. Lily's adventures had covered her in mud, slug slime, scratches, bruises, flea bites, and the faint smell of Gulliver's feet. Her palms were raw, her feet were sore, her ribs ached every time she breathed.

At last all the dirt and pain seemed to slide from her skin and into the hot, soapy water.

"I wanted to ask," Finn muttered from outside. "Why did you go upstairs without me?"

Lily scrubbed the slug slime from her hands. "I shouldn't have," she said. "But you were asleep, and I heard Dumpling with her friends. They were singing about Lilliput, Finn. I know it sounds impossible—"

"Were they singing rhymes?" he interrupted. "Like this?"

And he launched into a song:

> Gulliver, Gulliver,
> You're crazy as can be,
> Your brain's been pickled by the brine in the sea.
> Horses don't talk and
> Islands don't fly.
> Ghosts don't speak to passersby.
> Gulliver, Gulliver,
> Can you explain?
> Why don't the little people drown in the rain?
> Why don't the giants come and gobble us for tea?
> Gulliver, you're crazy
> As can be.

Lily was flabbergasted. "Yes!" she cried eventually. "Exactly like that! How do you know them too?"

"Everyone knows those rhymes," Finn answered. "All the children in the city. They were invented many years ago. I don't know when, or why."

"When Gulliver first came back from his travels." Lily suddenly understood. "To make fun of him. When he first told London about Lilliput no one believed a word. He brought back some Lilliputian sheep and cattle, but they all got eaten by rats. That's why he went back and fetched me. He needed proof."

Finn nodded. "I suppose that makes sense. Lots of the rhymes call him a liar. Or a lunatic."

"Gulliver was humiliated. Everywhere he went children in the street must have sung those rhymes. And they still do today, but no one knows why. It was too long ago. Everyone has forgotten."

"That's right," said Finn. "Dumpling and her friends know the rhymes, but not the reason behind them. They repeat, but they don't understand."

"Like Señor Chitchat," Lily said, thinking of the parrot on his perch.

"¡No seas descarado!" he squawked out, ruffling his feathers indignantly.

"It all makes sense," Lily continued, ignoring the

149

bird. "They all thought I was a dolly when they saw me. And after that I made them think I was a fairy."

Finn chuckled. "I was the same, remember? It wasn't until I found your note that I knew the truth."

"You're not like them, Finn," said Lily fiercely. "You're my safekeeper."

He sighed. "Yes I am. So don't leave me again, all right? I can't keep you safe if you wander off without me."

"Don't worry," Lily said, stepping from the egg cup. "I've learned my lesson."

She wrapped herself up in a clean handkerchief Mr. Ozinda had left for her and looked down at the filthy, raggedy dress she had been wearing for moons. She left it by the egg cup, and went to the pile of clothes Plum-Thumb had dumped out of the wardrobe.

The clothes were still in a pile, like a huge blob of rainbow-colored paint. Lilac and lavender ball gowns, crimson soldier's tunics...even a judge's black robe and snow-white wig. Scattered over the floor were a dozen pairs of clogs, boots, and slippers.

Lily was speechless. She had walked around barefoot ever since outgrowing her old iron shoes.

Plunging her hands into the pile, Lily began trying on outfits. Nothing seemed to fit at first. She threw down a princess's dress (too fancy), and a royal robe (too long). She pranced around in a black cloak for quite a while, but eventually she threw that away with the others (too spooky).

In the end Lily mixed and matched. She chose a soldier's green and gold jacket, a pair of white silk trousers, and some blue jewelled slippers. Finally she poked Stabber through her belt and stepped out of the front door.

"What do you think?" she asked Finn shyly.

He grinned. "Marvelous!"

"¡*Estupendo!*" said Señor Chitchat.

"Let me see!" called Mr. Ozinda, coming into the room.

Lily gave him a curtsy, and he burst into applause.

"Wonder of wonders!" he breathed. "I still think I am dreaming when I see you."

Lily blushed.

"Now, I think, is time for us to talk." Mr. Ozinda leaned on the counter, eyes twinkling.

"*Chitchat!*" called the parrot. "*Chitchat!*"

Lily nodded and sat on the dollhouse porch. Finn and Mr. Ozinda seated themselves on stools either side of the counter, leaning close. Not wanting to miss out on learning a few new words, Señor Chitchat flew down onto his owner's shoulder and listened too.

And Lily began to speak.

25

Where & How

Lily told Mr. Ozinda everything. About Lilliput, about Gulliver, about Finn. Sometimes the Spaniard interrupted her with a "Where?" or "How?" but mostly he just sat there stroking Señor Chitchat and listening.

"So," he said, when at last she had finished. "You wish to go home, Lily."

She nodded. "If I can."

"If you can, you must!" Mr. Ozinda declared. "I know what it is like to be far from the ones you love. Mrs. Ozinda, the *amor* I adore, is sailing the Atlantic as we speak…"

He turned to look at a portrait above the fireplace, and Mrs. Ozinda—a tiny woman with eyes the color of steel—gazed lovingly back at him.

"I shall help all I can." The Spaniard dabbed his eyes with a handkerchief. "You have my word. I swear by

Spain. By my Dumpling. By chocolate itself!"

Lily smiled. That was a promise she could trust.

"Now I have two safekeepers," she said.

"¡Tres!" Señor Chitchat squawked. *"Three!"*

"We must all work together," Mr. Ozinda declared, stroking his parrot fondly. "Until we do, Lily remains a prisoner here."

Lily frowned. She might still be lost, but she wasn't a prisoner anymore. "Finn's already freed me."

Mr. Ozinda smiled, taking a chocolate pot and stirring it thoughtfully. "But you still feel trapped, do you not?"

She thought about what she'd said to Finn in the alleyway and nodded.

"So, how can you be free?"

Lily didn't have an answer. She sat for a long time trying to think of one. Then she remembered what she had learned from the Waste-Not Watch.

The world is full of cages, and not all of them are built with iron bars.

"Gulliver still has me trapped," she whispered. "Even though I'm here and he's in the attic."

"Yes," said Mr. Ozinda, filling up two cups and the thimble. "He has you imprisoned in a cage of questions."

Lily nodded. She understood. "Where is Lilliput?"

she whispered. "That's the question. And only Gulliver knows the answer."

"Ah!" said Mr. Ozinda, leaning forward and handing Lily her thimble. "You are right. Gulliver knows the way to Lilliput. He will lead us there!"

Lily looked in bewilderment at the Spaniard.

So this is what happens when you drink too much hot chocolate, she thought. *It rots your teeth, bloats your belly, and turns your brain to mush.*

Finn was obviously thinking the same. "Are you saying," he said slowly, "that we need to ask Gulliver for directions?"

"Ah!" said Mr. Ozinda, and one corner of his mouth upturned into a smile. "Not at all. If I am right he has already written them down for us."

Lily tilted her head in confusion. What was he talking about?

"The book!" Finn cried suddenly, making her jump.

"¡Libro!" cried Señor Chitchat.

"¡*Exactamente!*" said Mr. Ozinda, leaning back and folding his hands on his belly. "The book of Gulliver's travels."

"The answer was there all along," said Finn, smacking his palm to his forehead. "It was with you in the attic, Lily. I even saw it on his desk."

"If I am right," Mr. Ozinda said, "we must look in this book of travels. There, Gulliver will have written exactly where he discovered Lilliput. Perhaps there will even be a map."

"Mr. Ozinda, you're a genius," laughed Finn. "I can't believe we didn't think of this before!"

"I know why," Lily snapped. "Because it's blumber-crock, that's why. You two are crazy. If we try sneaking into the attic to read that book, Gulliver will catch us in an instant!"

"That is the least of our worries," said Mr. Ozinda. "There is a second question we must answer. Knowing where Lilliput is will not be enough. We must also know how you will get there."

Lily nodded. She thought back to when she had almost convinced herself that Finn would be able to get her home in a few giant strides. Now they needed a real answer.

"Couldn't we just sail there?" Finn said. He turned to Mr. Ozinda. "You said that Mrs. Ozinda sails the world—won't she take Lily?"

Mr. Ozinda nodded doubtfully. "Of course she would. But there is a problem—one that we are battling against, even now."

"What?" said Lily, although she felt that she already knew.

"You have many enemies in this city—not just Gulliver. Cruel clock makers, hungry cats, deep mud, curious children. But the most dangerous enemy of all is time."

Lily knew what Mr. Ozinda was saying. Lilliputians measured their lives in moons, not years. Lily was growing up twelve times faster than Finn. She was almost twelve moons old. Half her life had been spent with Gulliver. He had brought her so far from home that getting back would take a long, long time.

It was a terrifying thought. By the time Lily returned she might not recognize Lilliput at all.

Or—even worse—home might not recognize her.

"The day before I was snatched, my nana was sixty moons old," Lily said. "That's five of your giant years. Now she'll be sixty-six. What if I get home and she's not there? What if all my friends have grown up and forgotten me? Sailing is too slow. There must be another way, one that's faster!"

"You are right," said Mr. Ozinda. "There must be. We only need to think of it."

For a long time the three of them sat there. Wishing for things that could never be. Thinking of plans that could never work. Mr. Ozinda muttered his ideas to Señor Chitchat, who dismissed each one with the phrase: "No me preguntes, yo sólo soy un loro."

Finn just stared into space, thinking his thoughts.

Lily could see them behind his eyes. A hundred possibilities were soaring, like birds.

Like birds.

Lily jumped up so quickly she sploshed hot chocolate into her lap. She didn't care. Finn had the answer.

"You're a genius!" she cried, startling everyone.

Finn looked baffled. "But I didn't say anything."

Lily just laughed, her excitement building. "It wasn't what you said, but what you thought."

"I must admit, I am puzzled a bit." Mr. Ozinda said. "Finn has a plan?"

"He does," said Lily, jumping up and down on her armchair in excitement. "I saw it in his eyes!"

"Then tell us, Finn, tell us!"

But Finn just shrugged hopelessly, and in the end it was Lily who told them:

"We're going to find me a pair of wings. It's obvious—if I can't sail across the sea, I'll have to fly over it instead!"

Mr. Ozinda's eyes darted around as he thought. "It could work," he muttered. "It *could* work. But we need to find a bird."

"*Hola,*" said Señor Chitchat.

"Not you," Mr. Ozinda told the parrot. "You can barely fly across this room, let alone an ocean. No, we need a special bird... There must be millions of birds in this city, and most of them won't do."

"Pigeon?" Lily suggested.

Finn shook his head. "Too stupid."

"Sparrow, then."

Mr. Ozinda made a *pfff* sound. "Too small and weak."

Lily's eyes sparkled. "An eagle!"

"Too rare," said Finn. "And too dangerous."

Lily sighed. "I don't know any other birds."

Finn gasped. "I do," he whispered with wide eyes. "I know just the bird we need. A *swift*."

"Pfff," said Mr. Ozinda again. "The swifts have all migrated south."

"But I know one that hasn't," said Finn. "And I know just where we can find him—he's in Mr. Plinker's workshop, trapped in the Astronomical Budgerigar. Mr. Plinker caught him roosting in the chimney. He was just being used to make sure the clock worked until Mr. Plinker bought a budgerigar. Then, after the accident, Mr. Plinker just left him there."

Lily leaped from her seat, her hand falling down to grip Stabber. Suddenly it all fell into place.

She knew what they had to do next.

"So it's Gulliver and Plinker," she said. "Plinker and Gulliver. They've got the answers. The answers to *Where?* and *How?* And we're going to get them."

26

Autumn & August

Lily rubbed her eyes, looking around at the tired faces of her friends. Light spilled in through the windows and onto the floor in slabs of golden syrup. Everyone looked exhausted.

"So," Lily asked drowsily. "What now?"

"The sun is dawning," said Mr. Ozinda, "and you are yawning, and we are as tired as can be. We will not rescue Swift this morning, so sleep, and I'll see you for tea."

"*Beddy-bye*," croaked Señor Chitchat, tucking his head under his wing.

But Lily didn't want to sleep.

"I'm not tired." She yawned, staggering up from her chair. "We've got a book to steal, and a bird to set free!"

"But, Lily," Mr. Ozinda said. "We cannot just rescue Swift with a click of our fingers. First we need a plan. There is thinking to be done, understand?"

She sank into her chair, grumbling. "I'm not going to sleep. You can all sit back and snore. Not me. I'm staying awake."

Mr. Ozinda shook his head and silenced her with a squawk. Lily looked up at him, startled. Then he sprouted gray feathers like Señor Chitchat and started laying chocolate eggs on the counter.

Oh well, Lily thought. *If I'm already dreaming, I might as well carry on.*

Over on the counter one of the chocolate eggs hatched a tiny chocolate chick. Lily fed him on cocoa beans, and he started to grow. When he was big enough, she jumped on his back and up they flew.

With a flap of the chocolate bird's wings they left London behind. Suddenly Lily was halfway to Lilliput, soaring over the seas, higher and higher. The world whirled beneath her and sweat dripped from the bird as she flew him faster and faster.

He's not sweating. He's melting! Lily realized with a jolt.

And then she knew—they were too high, too hot, too close to the sun. The chocolate bird melted away to nothing, and Lily fell from the sky and the dream with a *bump.*

She sat up on the floor of the dollhouse, next to the bed. Finn or Mr. Ozinda must have tucked her in when she was asleep. Kicking off the tangle of covers, she shivered. How quickly that dream had become a nightmare.

It wasn't just a nightmare, she told herself. It was a warning. We need to steal Swift and the Book of Travels without getting caught. If we don't have a good plan, everything will just melt away.

Lily stood up; she was jittery and restless. Every part of her wanted to rush to Plinker's Timepieces right now, but she knew they had to wait until they were ready.

Out in the chocolate shop Finn was still asleep. His snores made the curtains flutter. Lily poked her head out of the dollhouse window and spotted him across the counter curled up in an armchair.

"Rise and shine, it's half past nine!" she yelled at him in her best impression of Mr. Ozinda.

Finn gave a groan and forced himself awake. He looked at the clock above the counter. "Half past nine?" he moaned. "We've barely slept…"

"You giants are lazy," Lily grumbled. "You might live longer than Lilliputians but you spend it all snoring."

Up on his perch Señor Chitchat gave an irritated snort and buried his head deeper into his feathers.

Lily went down the stairs, buttoning up her sleeves and combing her hair with her fingers. As she stepped out onto the counter Mr. Ozinda thudded down the stairs in an enormous wine-colored nightgown.

"Good morning, Mr. Ozinda," she called to him. "Did you sleep well?"

"It was more a nap than a sleep," he sighed. "Never mind. I will mix a little coffee into our hot chocolate." He went to the window and threw it open. A few brittle leaves blew inside, and a cold breeze shook everyone awake.

"What's that smell?" said Lily, sniffing the air. "Like mud mixed with smoke?"

Mr. Ozinda lit the stove and began to clear the counter. "That, Lily, is the smell of autumn. It is August, you see. Summer is ending."

"Autumn," she breathed. The last time autumn had come was eleven moons ago—Lily had been a baby! The thought startled her. Time was moving so fast. The world was turning and the seasons were slipping away.

"Let's get to work on a plan," she said.

"Ah," said Mr. Ozinda. "First we must work on our appetites!"

Lily frowned. "What?"

"No time for questions!" said Mr. Ozinda. "We have already missed breakfast. I must hurry—there is barely time for brunch!"

He dashed off to the pantry and came back with his arms full of eggs, butter, bacon, and bread. Finn's eyes were wide with delight.

"Why are we eating?" Lily said anxiously. "Swift is stuck in that clock, and the Book of Travels is stuck in the attic... Shouldn't we—?"

"Of course we must plan," Mr. Ozinda said, coming back from the pantry again, this time with a bag of apples, half a dozen oysters, a wheel of cheese, and a lobster. "Planning is very important. For example...shall we have lobster for lunch, or supper?"

"Let's have it now!" Finn cried.

"Lobster for brunch? Don't be so silly! Tell me, what would you like, Lily?"

But Lily just stood there, fists clenched, lips pressed together. "I don't want anything," she said, trying to keep her temper. "Just a few crumbs and a drop of water. That's all."

Mr. Ozinda's moustache drooped a little. "But surely you—?"

"I said, no thank you!" Lily shouted, not caring that she was being rude. "I don't want breakfast, or brunch, or anything! It's almost autumn, you silly quogs! Don't you see?" Her voice cracked. "Almost autumn!"

She stomped over the counter and sat down on the

edge with her legs dangling over the side, hot and angry. What lazy, greedy safekeepers she had. All they cared about was snoring and stuffing their faces. Had they forgotten Lily was trying to get home? That her deadliest enemy was time?

"Here," said Finn, holding out a thimble for her to drink.

Lily ignored him. She just sat and gazed out of the window at the crystal-clear sky, at the soldiers on plumed horses trotting crisply around the square, at the leaves spinning away from the trees.

"I wish I could see in your eyes what you see in mine," Finn said softly. "Then I'd know what your worries were. I'd know what to say to make you feel better."

Lily looked down at her toes. "I'm trying to be patient," she said. "But I can't stop thinking about time. It ticks away so slowly for you, and so quickly for me. I just want the plan to be ready *right now*. I can't bear wasting time."

Finn bit his lip and nodded. He smiled at her, but his eyes were sadder than Lily had ever seen them.

"I understand." Then he turned and went back behind the counter.

Lily stayed gazing out the window, trying to solve the puzzle of his eyes. Why were they so sad?

Because once we rescue Swift and get Gulliver's book, I'll be leaving. I'll never see him ever again.

She felt a pang of guilt. Finn and Mr. Ozinda weren't wasting time at all. They were cherishing the few precious moments they had left with her.

Lily whirled back around, ready to blurt out an apology. She was being so selfish. But Finn was already suggesting a dozen different plans, and Mr. Ozinda was quietly stacking the food back into his pantry.

He said, "Without further ado, there is planning to do."

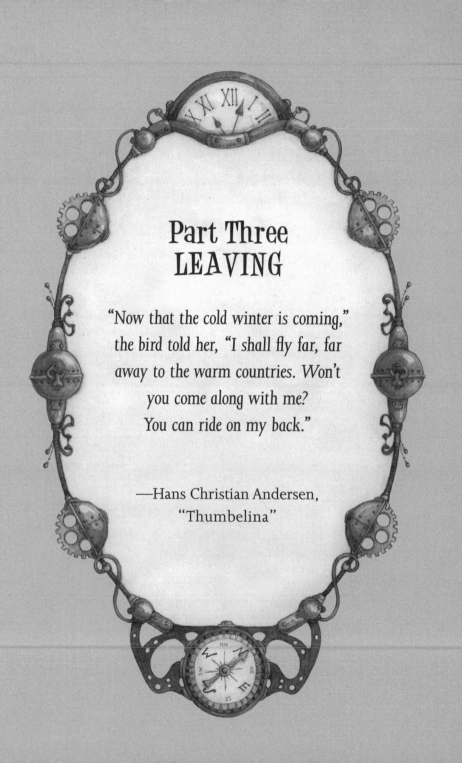

Part Three
LEAVING

"Now that the cold winter is coming,"
the bird told her, "I shall fly far, far
away to the warm countries. Won't
you come along with me?
You can ride on my back."

—Hans Christian Andersen,
"Thumbelina"

27

Planning & Preparation

For the rest of the day they worked like slaves. Finn scribbled diagrams on napkins, and Mr. Ozinda arranged truffles on the counter as if they were pieces in some enormously complicated board game.

Again and again, hour after hour, they thought of new risks and devised new solutions. Slowly the three of them began to form a plan—it was a daring rescue, a stealthy burglary, and a cunning getaway, all in one.

The plan involved Mr. Plinker's chimney, Mr. Ozinda's rhymes, a trout, and, most importantly, Señor Chitchat. If it worked, then Lily would be flying home on Swift before the morning.

If it failed and Lily was caught, she would be back in Gulliver's hands. Or, worse, Mr. Plinker's.

Around midday, two coaches pulled up to the doors of the chocolate shop, which Mr. Ozinda had kept closed to his customers. Plum-Thumb came miserably down the stairs and left clutching Princess Henry. Slug-Nose followed her with Mrs. Ittle-Wittle, glancing at Lily nervously, one hand reaching down every few seconds to check that she wasn't sprouting a Trufferdunk's tail.

"Won't they tell someone that they have seen me?" Lily wondered as Slug-Nose and Plum-Thumb went back to their homes.

Mr. Ozinda shrugged. "I have told them not to. But I imagine they will."

Lily started pacing the counter in worry, but then she realized—it didn't matter who Slug-Nose and Plum-Thumb told. No one would believe a word.

Finn smiled, but his eyes filled with sadness again. "Even if they do tell someone, and even if that someone believes them, it won't matter. You'll already be long gone."

Lily instantly felt guilty again and, as they were making such good progress with the plan, she insisted on stopping for lunch. The three of them dipped buttered toast into soft-boiled eggs, while Dumpling sulked and spied on them from the top of the stairs.

After moons and moons of eating bland porridge Lily had forgotten how tasty lunch could be. After saying thanks to the Ender, she gobbled up a whole yolk and a dozen crumbs of toast, until she was full to bursting.

"Wonderful lovely." She licked the butter from her fingers and looked up. Over the gravelly scrape of knives on toast she heard Finn laughing.

"What's so funny, Finn?"

"You're eating your egg upside down." He grinned. "The big end is meant to go at the bottom!"

"No it isn't." Lily sat up indignantly. "Lilliputians always crack their eggs this way."

"But why?"

"Because of the Ender."

"Who?"

"The Ender, Finn." Lily sighed and explained, "Whenever Nana gave me eggs for lunch she told me the story of how the Ender made the world. Do you want me to tell you too?"

Finn nodded, and so Lily began. It was the first story she had told outside of the Sock.

"In the time before time," she began, "the Ender sat in His cosmic kitchen and decided to make His dinner.

"First He lit the sun, which was His stove. Then He poured a jug of water, and that become the sea. Then He shook a bag of flour, and that became the land. He added a drop of milk, which became the moon, and a sprinkle of sugar, which became the stars.

"Then, at last, the Ender took two eggs, and cracked them at the big end, and something strange happened. Out hatched the very first people, and their names were Blefus and Lill.

"'Don't eat us!' they pleaded, and though the Ender was very hungry, and though the world He had made looked very tasty indeed, the Ender was kind. So He took pity on Blefus and Lill, and gave His world to them instead, for them to look after."

Finn grinned. "For safekeeping," he said.

Lily laughed. "I suppose so. That's why we Lilliputians always crack our eggs from the big end. To remind ourselves: we all came from kindness. We all sprang from the same place. The world is a gift."

After lunch Finn went out with a few coins to buy the things they needed for the plan. Lily wanted to go too, but Mr. Ozinda wouldn't allow it.

"It is no good just having the perfect plan," he told her. "You must be perfect too. It will be a long and dangerous journey, Lily, and we will not be there to help you. If you are not ready, you will not survive."

And so Mr. Ozinda made Lily copy out maps of the stars on square scraps of paper, and Señor Chitchat taught her a few basic phrases in Swiftian—"Time to fly," "Danger," "Keep together," and "Help!"

Lily listened to the shrill calls and whistles, over and over. Soon she found it easy to chirp along with Señor Chitchat.

"Chipchip, tsik, kee eeip," she called. "Skee, skee."

Mr. Ozinda grinned. "I have never seen someone parrot a parrot so well!"

Then they made a list of Lily's supplies.

"So," Mr. Ozinda said, rummaging around the chocolate shop. "You need food and water. And something to keep the warm in and the wet out, yes?"

Lily and Swift would have to seek shelter from anything stronger than a pitter-patter, but to keep off a light drizzle she found a miniature umbrella in the dollhouse wardrobe. For the cold nights Mr. Ozinda gave her one of his blue silk handkerchiefs as a blanket. For food he gave Lily an enormous chocolate truffle.

"That is a hundred dinners in a neat little ball!" he said. "Just make sure you do not scoff it all at once. You know why? You will get too fat for Swift to fly!"

"What will I drink, though?" Lily asked. "I'll parch without a drop of something."

"Ah!" Mr. Ozinda answered. "I have given this much thinking. And this is what I have thought."

He produced what looked to Lily like a splinter, but was in fact a tiny piece of...

"Straw?" she wondered. "What do I need straw for?"

"Ah," said Mr. Ozinda. "Because you do not need to take water. There is plenty of it hanging up in the sky."

"You mean clouds?" said Lily.

"That is exactly what I am meaning! Clouds are just very tiny drops of water, no? Tiny drops that we giants cannot drink. But you, Lily, are different...whenever you are thirsty you can fly up to the clouds and suck up the mist with this straw, yes?"

And so, thanks to Mr. Ozinda, Lily had everything she needed. But that created another problem.

"Where am I going to put it all?" she asked when the equipment was laid out in front of her. "Swift doesn't have any pockets, you know."

The answer was obvious, really. It would take many moons to fly back to Lilliput, and Lily needed somewhere to sit.

She needed a saddle. With saddlebags.

So, once Finn returned from the market, Lily made him dust great clumps of spider silk from the attic ceiling. Then she patiently untangled every strand and, using a splinter, wove them together into a harness with a seat and stirrups.

As the sun drifted down slowly from the sky, Mr.

Ozinda lit the hearth, and they all sat in the molten light of the fire, sewing and untangling. As they worked, Lily told her safekeepers about home.

She told them about the emperor's palace at Belfaborac; and the great city of Mildendo; about the little pebble and twig-thatch houses in the village of Plips; and the turtle shell on the Southern Beach, which was Lily and Nana's home.

She told every sad and happy story she could remember. She told *When the Rains Washed Mama and Papa Away*, and *When the Seagull Plopped on Nana*.

"It just fell from the sky like a big ball of smelly snow," Lily giggled. "And, *splat*! It covered Nana, right up to her neck! We had to dig her out with a shovel!"

"You remember so much," Finn said, with a hint of envy. "You were only six moons old."

"Memories are all I've got," said Lily as she sewed the last stitch. "If I forget them home really is gone forever. There! It's done!"

The saddle was a beautiful thing, with a light harness to loop around Swift's head. On either side of the seat, two pouches held the truffle and the star maps and blanket. There was a scabbard big enough to keep Stabber, her umbrella, and the straw.

In a flash of inspiration Finn had pulled a feather

from Señor Chitchat, which Lily had carefully stuck down onto the sticky spider silk to make the softest cushion.

"Nice and comfy," Lily said, testing it out. "It'll be a long journey...too long to put up with bum blisters."

She stepped off the saddle and admired it again.

Now all I need is the bird, she thought, and felt herself almost float up through the ceiling in joy.

But then the sadness gripped her by the ankles and pulled her back to the ground again, for the simple truth was that if their plan worked, Lily would go home and Finn would stay here in London.

Soon they would be saying good-bye.

28

Up & Away

At last the plan was ready and Lily had everything she needed to start her long journey home. But still she waited with her safekeepers in the chocolate shop. For Lily, Finn, Mr. Ozinda, and Señor Chitchat were about to become thieves, and they needed the cover of darkness.

As the evening drew on everyone grew nervous and restless. In an effort to chase away the gloom Mr. Ozinda stoked the fireplace and lit every candle, so that the shop was soon blazing with light. Lily and Señor Chitchat practiced over and over again the line that the parrot needed to speak in order for the plan to work:

> *Run, run as fast as can be,*
> *Gulliver's a yahoo and he'll never catch me!*

When it was perfect, Lily practiced her Swiftian and sharpened Stabber on the marble counter. The parrot took to reciting the alphabet in Spanish.

Finn was the only one who didn't fiddle or chatter. He packed a bag with all the equipment they needed, then sat by the window, watching the sun slip from the sky. His stillness rippled out to the others, until one by one they all fell into a brooding silence.

When there was no use in waiting any longer, Lily pushed her feet into her slippers, poked Stabber through her jacket, and hopped into Finn's waistcoat. Mr. Ozinda wrapped himself up in his cloak, put Señor Chitchat on his shoulder, and lit an oil lamp to lead them through the dark.

"Darling, my Dumpling, my sweet little something!" he called up the stairs. She appeared at the door a moment later, twisting her hair nervously with her fingers.

"Get on your coat, slip on your shoes! Quick, we have not a moment to lose!"

"Where are we going, Papa?" Dumpling whined as he prodded her out the door. "Papa?"

"¡Silencio!" Señor Chitchat squawked, and Lily and her safekeepers continued the rest of the journey without a word, each of them (except Dumpling, who knew nothing) rehearsing the plan in their heads.

Mr. Ozinda held up his lamp and started to waddle across St James's Park. A few carriages clattered over the square, and the soldiers by the palace all stood at attention.

A light drizzle came and spattered the pavement as they walked.

Lily huddled in Finn's pocket, afraid—rain could be deadly to Lilliputians. A sudden downpour could drown even the strongest of them. It had been a storm that had swept away Mama and Papa when Lily had been just a moonchild.

As the drizzle faded away and the skies above London cleared, Lily looked up at her safekeeper. If the plan worked, then the next time it rained the two of them would be far apart. This was the last time she could hide in Finn's pocket. After tonight it would just be her and Swift in the vast and lonely sky.

Eventually they reached Tock Lane, a street so narrow that at points Mr. Ozinda had to squeeze down it sideways. As they passed the workshops of the other clock makers, Lily heard the steady tick-tock, tick-tock, tick-tock from inside each one.

The houses and the minutes flew past until, at last, they arrived at a crooked, damp house with darkened windows and a faded sign swinging above the door that said *Plinker's Timepieces*.

"Something's stinky, Papa," Dumpling grumbled. "I don't like it."

"It's not something," whispered Finn. "It's some*one*."

Lily looked up nervously at the three floors—first Mr. Plinker's workshop, then the bedroom where he slept, then the tiny attic window, poking out from the roof tiles.

"Ready?" said Finn. He reached in his pocket to lift Lily out, but she elbowed his fingers away.

"Wait," she said. "Listen."

Plinker's Timepieces didn't sound like the other workshops. It was almost silent. There was not a single tick-tock.

"The clocks have all stopped," Finn murmured. "Mr. Plinker isn't patient enough to keep winding them up."

"It's not the clocks I'm listening for," Lily whispered. "It's him."

And suddenly there came a faint cry: *"Skee, skee..."*

"There!" she said, clambering up Finn's arm. "Did you hear that? Swift, calling for help!"

Lily trembled all over as she jumped onto Mr. Ozinda's shoulder. "Scoot up," she told Señor Chitchat, who ruffled his feathers and tutted.

She waited as Finn pulled open the bag and began handing out the equipment. Swift's saddle for Lily; a reel of thread for Señor Chitchat; a fat gray trout wrapped in old leather skin for Dumpling. Lily winced, holding her nose against the stench.

"Horatio's favorite fish," Finn said.

"I don't want to hold it, it's all slimy," Dumpling complained, grasping the trout by the tail. "And it *smells*."

"Of course it smells." Finn grinned. "I bought the stinkiest trout I could find. Horatio will be able to catch a whiff of it from a mile away."

"I hope so," said Lily.

She looked around. All her safekeepers had fallen silent. They had their equipment. They were ready. Now they were waiting for her to give the word.

"Remember," she told them. "Gulliver, Mr. Plinker, and Horatio are in there. If this plan is going to work, they all need to be lured out here onto the street. That's your job. Leave Swift and the *Book of Travels* to me."

Everyone nodded, and though she was more nervous than she had ever been in her life, Lily smiled at each of them. Finn, Mr. Ozinda, Señor Chitchat. She even gave a grudging nod to Dumpling.

"And I want to say thank you," she said. "You're not just my safekeepers, you're my friends. You've given me so much."

She looked at Finn and said, "You gave me hope."

She looked at Señor Chitchat and said, "And a way home."

She looked at Mr. Ozinda. "And hot chocolate!"

Lastly she looked at Dumpling, who bit her lip and

looked down at her toes. "And a headache," Lily grinned, remembering her fall down the stairs.

She stopped herself there. It felt too much as if she were saying good-bye forever. A good-bye (especially a good-bye forever) is a heavy thing, and Lily didn't want to feel weighed down. Not when Señor Chitchat was just about to carry her up to the chimney.

So she just nodded to each of them, wrapped her arms tight around the parrot's foot, and said: "Up and away!"

"*Up and away*," Señor Chitchat repeated. "*Up and away.*"

And, flapping his wings, they soared into the air.

29

Mimic & Miracle

Lily held her breath as Finn, Mr. Ozinda, and Dumpling shrank to the size of dolls and the rooftop appeared. It was like another world; another London. No reek and clamor up here, just the moon shining and the stars twinkling and the smoke plumes curling up into the night. Cold and peaceful. Hushed.

She hung onto Señor Chitchat as he struggled up and up, with the reel of thread in his claws, until finally he perched on the top of chimney.

"*Phew!*" he croaked.

"Well done, Chitchat." Lily stroked his chest. The parrot puffed up with pride.

She hopped from his leg and put down her saddle. They were very high. A gust of wind whistled in her ears and disappeared with a moan down the flue. Lily tried not to look down.

She held out her hand over the chimney. There was no heat or smoke at all. That meant no fire in the attic below.

Just as Lily had expected. Now that she was gone, Gulliver hadn't bothered to light the hearth.

She smiled. He had always expected her to escape up the chimney, but now she was about to climb down it.

"Ready?" she asked Señor Chitchat.

As the parrot bobbed his head, Lily caught a glimpse of something behind him. She drew Stabber from her belt. A shadow was slinking across the rooftop in their direction.

Horatio padded silently over the tiles toward his dinner, which was behaving very strangely indeed.

Usually the birds Horatio hunted were sparrows and starlings. Slender, timorous little things, all fury and no flesh. They pecked at breadcrumbs and were startled by the wind. They were very hard to catch.

This bird, though, was enormous—half as big as Horatio himself. And he didn't fly away at all. He watched Horatio pawing closer, and then he said, *"Get away from my guest, you pest!"*

Horatio hesitated. There were three things he liked to do with his dinner—hunt it, play with it, and eat it. But so far hunting the strange bird had been disappointing, and a little unnerving. Playing with him would be a challenge. Eating him might become a chore. After all, he was rather big.

It was then that Horatio spotted that his dinner also came with dessert. A little, tasty-looking shadow moved just below the bird.

Horatio gave a purr, and then shrank back—it was the creature from yesterday, the thing with the silver sting! He saw it glint in moonlight and hissed, his paw throbbing with the memory.

Horatio slunk back. Fighting with his dinner was not something he enjoyed.

Suddenly his nose twitched. He could smell something else. It was so strong and so delicious that Horatio could *see* it hanging in the air. A rippling silver thread, with flashes of green and a tinge of pink.

Horatio turned and followed the smell down to the street. He leaped from the gutter to a windowsill then dropped onto the sidewalk. The smell wafted from an alleyway, and he hung his head, expecting the stray cats (who were bigger than Horatio) and the sewer rats (who were biggest of all) to be there already. But to his surprise there was only a small girl.

"Here, kitty-kitty," she said. In her hand dangled a glistening, silver trout.

Horatio began to purr. Trout was his favorite. He forgot completely about the strange bird, and the thing with the silver sting up on the roof. He didn't even notice when, high above him, Señor Chitchat started to speak.

In the attic Gulliver kneeled by his bed, alone and desperate. Since waking yesterday afternoon and finding Lily gone he had fallen into despair. He did not know where she was, or how to get her back.

"Please, Lily," he whispered. "Please, come back to me."

Lemuel Gulliver was a man of science. He believed in reason. He believed in progress. He did not believe in prayers. Or miracles. Or gin.

And so it was highly unusual for him to be drunk, with his hands clasped together, asking for the impossible to happen.

And it was even more unusual for Lily to suddenly answer him.

There was a *tap, tap, tap* at the window. Gulliver sat up on his elbows, his long hair drizzling down onto his shoulder.

Then he heard her voice:

Run, run, as fast as can be,
Gulliver's a yahoo and he'll never catch me!

Señor Chitchat's impression of Lily was a little squawky, but Gulliver was full of gin, and empty of hope. He leaped to his feet.

"Lily?" he hiccupped. "Lily, is that you?"

And he heard again:

Run, run, as fast as can be,
Gulliver's a yahoo and he'll never catch me!

"You are alive!" he said, crying tears of joy. "You have come back! Oh, Lily, I have been so worried..."

He flung open the window, but there was nothing there. Señor Chitchat had already flown back to the chimney.

"Lily, where are you?" Gulliver called. "Come back, please!"

He lit a lantern, pulled on his coat, and burst out of the attic. Then he clomped down the stairs and onto the street, leaving his Book of Travels lying open on the desk.

30

Lure & Limerick

L ily smiled to herself as she watched her kidnapper disappear down Tock Lane, calling out her name.

Well, she thought. *Horatio is chasing a fish and Gulliver is chasing a parrot. That just leaves Mr. Plinker.*

Lily strained her ears, trying to hear the clock maker down the chimney. He was somewhere in there. She could smell his stink.

Lily fretted nervously, pacing around the chimney pot, looking down at the street. Of all their plan this part was the riskiest. The one she felt most worried about. Because there were only two things that Mr. Plinker would leave his workshop for.

Finn or Lily. Lily or Finn.

He had already chased after them once before. Finn was almost more valuable to the clock maker than his own fingers. Mr. Plinker needed an apprentice to wind up his clocks and make them tick.

Lily gazed down at the street below as Finn crept up to the front door of the workshop. He was the bait. She tried to remember that Finn was fast and clever. She tried to remember that Mr. Ozinda was down there too—it was his job to protect Finn if something went wrong.

But as she was trying to remember, Lily was also trying to forget—she was trying to forget that Mr. Plinker had already caught Finn once before.

She shook her head, annoyed with herself. It was too late to worry now. Finn was already right outside the workshop, singing a rhyme.

> There once was a man from Tock Lane,
> Whose clocks were completely insane.
> He just couldn't fix
> All their tocks and their ticks
> His apprentice, I think, is to blame.

Mr. Ozinda had come up with it. He said that it would be so irritating to hear, Mr. Plinker would have to chase Finn.

Lily couldn't wait to see if he was right or not. Now was her chance. She had a Book of Travels to steal and a Swift to set free.

"Keep Finn safe," Lily whispered to the Ender.

She checked that her saddle was tied tight around her waist, and that the reel of thread was still looped around Señor Chitchat's foot.

"You did brilliantly with Gulliver," she told Señor Chitchat. "Now, remember—don't fly away. You're my rock!"

"*Soy tu roca,*" the parrot said.

Lily gulped, hoping that meant he understood. Then, like a fisherman with his bait, Señor Chitchat dangled Lily above the chimney. Slowly she lowered down into the pool of blackness.

As Lily rappelled down the chimney and Finn stood outside the workshop, Mr. Plinker was at his counter working. When he heard the voice of his runaway apprentice drift into the room, he did not rant and rave and foam at the mouth in rage.

Instead he began to laugh. Very quietly, so that Finn would not hear.

Then he said to himself, "What perfect timing."

And it was.

Mr. Plinker took the clock he had just been fixing from the counter. He slipped the Waste-Not Watch in his pocket and listened to Finn outside. He did not know why his apprentice had come back, only that he was there.

Soon Finn would once again be Mr. Plinker's apprentice. His prisoner. His slave.

Silently Mr. Plinker slipped his feet into his shoes. His coat rustled onto his arms. He slithered out of the workshop and into the shadow at the top of the stairs. He stood there, utterly still. Observing Finn. Like a crocodile in a swamp observes his prey.

Slowly, keeping in the dark, Mr. Plinker began to creep down the stairs.

Closer.

Closer.

At last, he was at the front door.

Finn was out on the street, still singing Mr. Ozinda's irritating limerick. The clock maker put his left hand on the handle. Then he reached above the door with his right and muffled the little bell that jingled whenever a customer came in.

Slowly, slowly, slowly, he began to turn the handle and open the door.

31

Map & Trap

L ily went deeper down the chimney, while above her the little square of starry sky shrank to the size of a stamp.

She rehearsed the plan in her head. First she was heading to the attic to steal the *Book of Travels*. Then she would go down the stairs to Mr. Plinker's workshop and rescue Swift.

The inky dark around her started to fade, and she saw a pile of ashes on a ledge below her feet. The attic fireplace! When she had last been here it had been a mass of glowing coals—an impassable volcano.

Now, though, the fire was just a mountain of ashes and the attic was lit by candles.

Lily lowered herself until she twirled a few inches above the hearth. She untied the thread and dropped, skidding down the cinders to the bottom.

The attic was just as she remembered, only now it looked smaller. There was her birdcage, swinging empty on its hook. There was the rusty nail, halfway into the doorframe. Gulliver's mess. His bed.

His desk.

That's where I'll find it, she thought.

Carefully Lily sniffed the air. Mr. Plinker's stink wasn't so strong now. He must have left the workshop. She listened out in the street for him but heard nothing. She hoped that was a good sign. She hoped Finn was all right.

With the saddle tied around her shoulders, Lily jumped down onto the floorboards, looking for a way up to the Book of Travels. It didn't take long.

She climbed a stack of old plates onto Gulliver's bed and dragged an old fork over the space between the desk and the mattress. She stepped across it like a tightrope walker.

Pressed into the candle wax on the desk were her footprints from two nights ago, like fossils from another time. The Book of Travels lay to one side. It still smelled faintly of coffee and some of the edges were singed. Lily scrambled up the stack of paper and stood on the first page.

Now came the hard part: finding the chapter of the book she needed. The bit that told her where Lilliput was.

Lily walked back and forth, wondering where to start. She opened the book to a random page.

She read, "It is computed that eleven thousand persons have at several times suffered death rather than submit to break their eggs at the smaller end."

I'm wasting time, she thought. This chapter isn't telling me anything useful.

She turned back to page one. Gulliver started by writing about his life: after his studies he had come to London to become a doctor and study medicine. He had got married. His wife's name was Mary.

That had all been hundreds of moons ago, back when it had been the year 1699, before Nana's nana had been born. Now it was 1720. Lily wondered where Mary was now. Gulliver had never mentioned her, not once.

Maybe she had died while he was on his travels, or maybe he had just shut himself away from her, like he had from everyone else.

Lily turned the page. She had always thought of Gulliver as her kidnapper. But once, long ago, he had been more than that. He had been a doctor. A husband. A father.

Now he wasn't anything. Just a lonely, locked-up man who was a long way from home. As Lily stood there, she suddenly felt sorry for him. It shocked her. She never thought she could pity Gulliver. Not after what he had done. But she could see now—even though he had kept her in a cage, he was the real prisoner.

Wandering over the sentences, Lily tugged a loose page from the book and froze. There was a drawing—squiggled coastlines with tiny labeled names. She was standing on a map.

Heart beating fast, Lily skipped over countries and coastlines until she let out a choked gasp. Down by her toes was a tiny blob of an island that Gulliver had neatly labeled Lilliput.

Soon I'll be standing on Lilliput for real, she told herself.

Trembling with excitement, she dragged the map to the edge of the desk. It was like an enormous, stiff rug—far too big to carry or drag.

So, using Stabber, Lily scored lines in the page and then folded them carefully. For the next few minutes, she worked silently, listening for any sound from the street that might signal the return of Gulliver. But there was nothing. Just the curtains rasping in the wind.

Lily pinned Stabber back onto her jacket and looked down at the paper with satisfaction. It was a map no longer—now it was an arrow-shaped glider. Picking it up, she took a few unsteady steps backward. Then she broke into a run, right to the edge of the desk and off...into nothingness.

As Lily floated in the attic, Finn fell in the street. Over him stood Mr. Plinker.

"Welcome back," said the clock maker.

Finn could not answer. He could not move. He was in shock. Everything had happened in a blur—Mr. Plinker's hand shooting from the door, Finn jerking back and tripping, a flash of something jagged closing around his arm like jaws...

He stared down in horror at his wrist.

The Waste-Not Watch was strapped on.

Tight.

And it was ticking.

"I fixed it, Finn," Mr. Plinker said in a wicked whisper. "I let all the other clocks wind down. I spent my time putting the Waste-Not Watch back together. I was going to go to the House of Safekeeping and buy another apprentice from Mother Mary Bruise. But then you came here and saved me the effort. And the money."

Finn turned around to call for help, but Mr. Ozinda was already there.

"You beast, you brute, you greasy-brained newt!" he said trembling all over. "Let Finn go."

Mr. Plinker narrowed his eyes to slits. "And who are you?" he asked the chocolate maker.

Mr. Ozinda did his best to look terrifying. "Let Finn go!" he repeated. "My fists insist!"

Finn looked over at Mr. Plinker. The clock maker didn't look frightened at all. In fact, he was laughing to himself.

Mr. Ozinda stepped forward, swinging his arms. "You'll regret your chuckles. Here—meet my knuckles!"

Mr. Plinker sidestepped him neatly, and Mr. Ozinda's punch went wide.

"I'll crunch you like a cookie!" the Spaniard huffed. "I'll slice you like a flan! I'll—"

There was a dull thwack as the clock maker punched Mr. Ozinda on the jaw. The Spaniard blinked once, wobbled, and collapsed onto the floor like custard.

"Pathetic," Mr. Plinker grunted as he rolled the Spaniard into the alleyway, out of sight.

"Mr. Ozinda!" gasped Finn. He scrambled to his feet and went to run, but then the hand on the watch traveled once around the clockface, and a tiny bell went ding-dong.

All by itself the buckle tightened. Finn cried out, trying to tug the Waste-Not Watch over his hand. It didn't even budge.

"I hope you now understand how important it is to obey me, Finn," the clock maker said from behind him. As Finn turned, Mr. Plinker held out the copper key that hung on his neck with string. "Remember, only

I can unwind the Waste-Not Watch. Do what I ask and I promise to stop the pain."

Ding-dong went the watch, tightening again.

Finn felt sick. Already the pain made his head swim. He couldn't escape. He couldn't do anything. Mr. Plinker had him trapped once more.

"What do you want?" he asked in a small voice.

A smile spread over Mr. Plinker's face, the way water ripples from a dropped stone.

"I want the Lilliputian," he said.

32

The Astronomical Budgerigar

Lily gripped the glider tight as it soared out of the attic door. She swerved right on the landing, then wobbled down the steps.

Air rushed in her face, and her stomach plunged as she went faster and faster. Then she tugged the glider to the left, whipped through the open doorway, and flew into the workshop.

Now that it was night, the room was much scarier. It was silent as a graveyard, messy as a slaughterhouse, gruesome as a torture chamber. Lily floated past the clocks. There was something ghoulish about their frozen faces, staring at her. Lifeless. Still.

She shivered. Mr. Plinker might be gone, but the stink of him was still so strong it made her want to gag. Her eyes darted around nervously as she reminded herself that the clock maker was off chasing Finn, not lurking here.

A sudden sound, halfway between a scream and sigh, made Lily wobble on the glider. It was so full of sadness it made her want to weep.

"Skee...skee..."

"Swift," Lily breathed.

She bit her lip with worry. His cries came from the counter, where the Astronomical Budgerigar sat. He sounded so weak. Finn hadn't been here to feed him since yesterday morning. What if he couldn't fly? He had been trapped for so long.

She spun the glider down onto the workbench in a tight corkscrew and skidded to a stop. Quickly she unfolded it back into a page, and taking Stabber she cut the map into tiny jigsaw pieces. An atlas. Stacked together they were the size and thickness of a Lilliputian book.

Lily tucked the atlas into one of the saddle pockets and hurried forward, past a teetering stack of old clocks. Somewhere at the other end of the counter, Swift called out for help.

"Skee! Skee! Skee!"

"Hold on!" she called out, trying to calm him. "I'm almost there! Just a little longer..."

Now she was close enough to see the Astronomical Budgerigar itself. Like everything else in the workshop, the clock had wound down. There was no point waiting for it to strike midnight and send Swift shooting out to call the time.

If Lily wanted to free him she would have to climb inside the clock and untie him from the perch.

"Skee!" came Swift's cry, more urgent than ever. "Skee! Skee!"

Lily looked above the square face of the Astronomical Budgerigar at the small window. It was made of glass, with brass hinges.

That's where the perch shoots out, when the clock chimes the hour. That's the best way in. Here goes...

Stepping onto a bundle of clock hands, Lily began to climb. There were plenty of footholds, because the wooden casing was so cracked. Soon she had hoisted herself up to the window above the clock face. Brushing the dust from the glass, she peered inside.

As her eyes adjusted to the gloom, Lily gasped.

The clock was a dingy ruin, but it was still breathtaking. As big as a cathedral, as complicated as a steam engine, as busy as a bee's nest. The window was open, just a sliver. But it was enough. Lily squeezed inside, wrinkling her nose at the smell of oil and smoke.

Dust lay thick on the floor, and long ropes of grease dangled and dripped from the center spoke. Mashed up

in the cogs were poor, squashed spiders that made her shiver. This was a terrible place to be trapped. It was deadly.

Away from the window a wide tunnel led down into the heart of the machine.

This is where the perch travels as it shoots from the clock, she told herself. *Swift will be at the end of this tunnel.*

Lily took a step forward, then another and another. Somewhere, a tiny bell jingled. She tensed, thinking that the clock might still be capable of ticking, but nothing happened.

Relax, she told herself. *Everything's going to plan. Just find Swift.*

The bird's calls echoed around the clock: "Tsik tsik!" he called. "Tsik tsik!"

She frowned. That sounded like a phrase Señor Chitchat has taught her, but Lily couldn't remember what it meant.

Behind her, hinges creaked and something went click. Lily spun around in a panic. Was the clock was winding up again?

"Tsik tsik!" Swift cried.

And Lily remembered—tsik in Swiftian meant *danger*! She ran back to the window. It was shut. She pushed, but it wouldn't budge. She flung herself against the glass, barging with her shoulder, beating with her fists.

She was locked in.

Behind her, Swift called out a sad, faint, "*Skee...*"

Tap tap tap. Lily whirled back to the door and jumped. Mr. Plinker's long brown nail was clinking against the glass. *Tap tap tap.* "Are you in there?" he said. "Are you in there, little one?"

33

Caged & Caught

M r. Plinker kneeled down, leering at Lily. The glass door was slightly warped, making his grin impossibly wide. It wrapped around her as he spoke.

"You fit!" the clock maker said delightedly. "You fit perfectly! Why, you are just the right size, I think. Not too big, and not too small."

Lily took a step back from the door. "Just the right size? For what?"

At this, Mr. Plinker began to giggle. "Why, to make my clocks, of course."

Lily stared at the clock maker, and saw herself reflected in his gaze. To Gulliver she had been a specimen. To Dumpling she had been a toy. But in Mr. Plinker's eyes she was nothing but a slave.

"Just think!" he continued rapturously. "You can build my inventions *from the inside out*...and that is just the start! Eventually, you will make clocks so tiny and delicate that they will seem more magic than machinery! And I will be the richest clock maker in all the world!"

Lily trembled, but she forced herself to look Mr. Plinker in the eye.

Stay brave, she told herself. *Keep him talking. There's still Finn and Mr. Ozinda outside. They'll rescue you.*

"How can I make you a clock?" she asked as bravely as she could. "I don't know anything about them."

Mr. Plinker began to giggle again. "But that's not quite true, is it?" he said. "You unwound my Waste-Not Watch, so I know you have talent. You will quickly learn the rest. Won't she, Finn?"

He stepped aside and behind him Finn answered: "Yes, Mr. Plinker."

Lily's head stung as if she had been slapped. She backed away from the window, stumbled, and fell. Something bad had happened. Something was very, very wrong. Her friend, her safekeeper...why was he back with Mr. Plinker?

At last Finn raised his head. His face was streaked with tears. He looked as if he were in agony, though Mr. Plinker had not so much as touched him.

"I'm sorry, Lily." Finn held up the Waste-Not Watch ticking on his wrist.

That's when Lily began to panic.

That's when she knew the plan had gone badly, badly wrong.

Out in the street, Gulliver's travels had led him to a little girl at last. But not the one he was expecting.

This little girl sat outside Plinker's Timepieces, stroking a ginger cat and talking to a huge mound of trash that was clogging up the gutter.

"Mr. Plinker is a stinker," she said.

Gulliver approached her warily. "Child?" he said softly.

The little girl lifted her head and stared at him. Her lip quivered, and the cat crouched down by her ankles and hissed.

Gulliver hesitated. It had been a long time since he had talked to anyone but Lily. But he was too full of gin and desperation for that to matter much now.

And so he blurted out, "Do you believe in fairies?"

The little girl sniffed and rubbed her little snout of a nose. "Yes," she said eventually. "You have to be nice to them, or they'll turn you into a trufferdunk."

She turned back to the mound of trash. "Mr. Plinker is a stinker. He's a beast and a brute and a greasy-brained newt."

"Well," said Gulliver, trying to interrupt her. "I am

looking for a fairy. Have you seen one?" He was very much puzzled as to why the little girl was talking to a trash pile.

"Slimy, smelly, awful man," she sang. "He messed up little Lily's plan."

Gulliver jumped and almost dropped his lantern. "You said Lily!" he cried, trying to keep calm. "You know her? Where is she?"

A second, even more exciting, realization struck Gulliver, and he jumped again. "Who are you talking to?" he asked. "Is there...someone in that gutter?"

"Yes," said the girl. "It's Papa. Mr. Plinker hit him on the head and made him sleep. I'm telling him rhymes. They always wake him up."

Shining his lantern at the gutter, Gulliver was startled to see that the mound of trash was actually a man. An enormous man, lying there with the slop and the trickling slime.

And, as Gulliver watched, he was even more startled to see the enormous man open his eyes.

"Who is that?" he groaned. "Lily and Finn...you must listen...plan has failed...rescue mission..."

It was not one of Mr. Ozinda's best rhymes, because he had just been punched in the head, and it left Gulliver feeling utterly confused.

"Rescue Lily? Where is she? Tell me! Please!"

But Mr. Ozinda could not manage another word, and when Gulliver turned to the man's daughter she just shrugged.

Fortunately, there was someone else in the room to explain.

Unfortunately, the explanation was in Spanish.

"*Hola*," said a voice from above.

"Well done, Finn," said Mr. Plinker in the workshop. "You have served me well tonight."

He inserted the copper key into the Waste-Not Watch and twisted it twice. The strap loosened just a little, just enough to lessen Finn's agony. He let out a whimper of relief.

"Relax, Finn," said the clock maker, trying to sound kind. "For a few moments, at least."

Lily wanted to scream. She wanted to cry. But screaming and crying wouldn't rescue them. Nothing could. They were all prisoners of Mr. Plinker's cruel imagination. First Swift, then Finn...and now her too.

"Where's Mr. Ozinda?" she shouted through the window's glass. "Where is he, Finn? Finn?"

Lily looked at him. He wouldn't answer, or even meet her eye. It was like he didn't know her anymore. It was like he was just another of Mr. Plinker's machines.

Lily threw herself against the glass window again and again, hurling every rude word she could think of at Mr. Plinker.

"You *zijji-gunching*, uck stinking *fluggytat!*" she bellowed, throwing herself against the window. "You yahoo! You *quog!* You *slubber!*"

Mr. Plinker smirked. "Call me what you like, but you are still my slaves. And now, it's time for you to start mending my clocks. You can start with the Astronomical Budgerigar. It has a nasty habit of trying to murder people. Fix it, and make it tick again."

"Never!" Lily shouted. "We'll never work for—"

But Finn's fingers interrupted her—they were already working on the Astronomical Budgerigar. Twisting and turning and tinkering.

"No, Finn!" Lily climbed through the clock and gave his thumb a kick. "Don't give in! Don't be his slave!"

"You need to go deeper inside the clock, Lily," he said, ignoring her pleas. "Doesn't she, Mr. Plinker?"

"Of course," said the clock maker. "Right into the middle, where Finn can't reach."

Lily collapsed by her safekeeper's hand, weeping

with rage and frustration. Her tears drifted through the clock, mingling with the dust.

"You can't give up," she sobbed. "You have to hope, Finn. You have to. That's what you told me."

His fingers stopped polishing a cog. The Waste-Not Watch tick-tick-ticked.

"Go deeper, Lily," said Finn at last. His voice wasn't weak or defeated, it was strong. Urgent. "Go deeper in. That's where you'll want to be when I wind up the clock."

Lily was about to call him an *oik*-smelling *mungle bof* when she realized—Finn wasn't ordering her around, he was trying to give her a message.

And suddenly she understood what it was.

34

Saddle & Swift

Finn, you're a genius!" Lily whispered, waving away her tears.

Now she knew what he was doing. How had it taken her so long to understand? Finn was fixing the Astronomical Budgerigar, but not for Mr. Plinker. He was doing it to set Lily free.

When the clock began to tick again, it would strike one.

And the glass window would spring open.

And Lily and Swift could escape.

Shuffling away from Finn's fingers, Lily climbed over the cogs until she stood back by the glass window. She tiptoed down the tunnel that descended into the heart of the Astronomical Budgerigar. The deeper she went, the darker it got.

Suddenly she stopped. Up ahead, a dark *something* was ruffling and shuffling. There. On a tiny perch.

"Swift," she breathed.

He was as fierce as a dragon, as wild as a storm, as helpless as a child. Leather straps bound his wings, chest, and feet to the perch. As Lily crept toward him, Swift turned to watch her, for his head was all he could move. He was a pitiful sight.

"*Skee, skee,*" he called.

Blinking away her tears, Lily answered him with one of the Swiftian phrases that Señor Chitchat had taught her.

"*Chip chip,*" she sang.

Time to fly.

Swift's dark eyes studied Lily, and he cocked his head. He was listening to her, but did he understand? Lily crawled closer, as close as she dared, and reached out her hand to touch him.

Swift cried out again and his beak stabbed toward her like a spear. She jerked back just in time.

He understands, but he doesn't trust me. I don't blame him. Lily remembered when Finn had come to free her from Gulliver. She had been terrified.

How could she make Swift trust her? He was a wild animal, scared and starving.

That gave her an idea. Reaching carefully between two cogs, she pulled out a squashed bit of spider.

"You must be hungry," Lily whispered, offering it up to his beak. "Go on, take it."

For a moment Swift gave her a puzzled look. Then he lunged out, pecked the spider leg from her hand, and swallowed it whole.

"I'm Lily." She reached out for him again. Swift shuddered, but this time he let her fingertips rest upon his feathers. They were sleek and smooth.

"I'm here to set you free," Lily whispered at last. "But first you have to put this on."

She brought up the saddle. Swift twisted away from her, but the leather straps held him trapped.

"Skee! Skee!"

"It's not going to trap you," Lily promised as she looped the harness over his head, fixing the saddle to the spot between his wings. "You won't even know it's on."

She leaned her head against his feathers, whispering to him in Swiftian until he calmed. Then she ventured back through the clock again, looking for more dead spiders in the cogs.

Mr. Plinker would think Lily was cleaning the clock, just as he had ordered. He wouldn't be able to see her feeding Swift. Making him stronger. Getting him ready to fly.

"You're up to something!" Mr. Plinker snapped, and it took Lily a moment to realize he couldn't see her—the clock maker was talking to Finn.

"I'm working as fast as I can," Finn said.

It was a lie. Lily knew. She heard the Waste-Not Watch ticking away almost constantly. Finn's teeth were grinding together as he tried to block out the pain. But, still, every few seconds he would pause to wipe the dust from his eyes and the sweat from his brow.

He was dawdling. Trying to give her more time.

Lily turned and fled back to Swift. The bird trembled as she went from his feet, to his chest, to his wings, undoing the leather straps that held him to the perch.

At last Finn couldn't waste another second. Just as Lily freed Swift's feet she heard her safekeeper say: "I have to test the clock hands now, Mr. Plinker. To see if they're damaged."

"Of course, of course," said the clock maker irritably. "Just hurry."

Above Lily the central spoke of the clock turned. A shower of dust fell down on her head, making her sneeze. Finn's voice echoed in her ears.

"Twelve o'clock...eleven o'clock..."

She understood at once—Finn was winding the clock hands back, an hour at a time.

It was a countdown.

"Ten o'clock...nine..."

"Come on!" Lily hissed at her fingers as they slipped and fiddled with the buckle.

"Eight...seven..."

Suddenly the strap came loose in her hands. All Lily had to do now was let go and jump on. Swift quivered, like an arrow in a bow, straining against her grip.

Wait, she told herself. *Wait until the last moment.*

"Six..."

If this doesn't work...

"Five..."

It will work.

"Four..."

It has to.

And Lily let go of the strap and jumped.

She landed on the saddle as Swift reared up. Now

that he was no longer tied down, Lily saw him for what he was. Wild. Fierce. Proud. With one flex of his wings, Swift tossed her from the saddle.

She toppled backward, slid down the feathers of his tail, and clattered into the cogs below the perch.

"Three…"

Desperately Lily scrambled to her feet, jumping up at the perch. But it was too late. In another second the clock would be wound. The Astronomical Budgerigar would strike one. The perch would shoot forward. Swift would fly from the clock without her.

"Two…"

And Lily would be ground up in the cogs like meat in a mincer.

"One," said Finn.

35

Sprugs & Sorrow

"Wait!" Mr. Plinker hissed. "Wait right there! What's that sound?"

Nothing happened. The pulleys didn't fall and the cogs didn't turn. Swift gripped his perch, looking for a way out, but there wasn't one.

Lily lifted herself free of the cogs, wondering what had happened. Did Mr. Plinker know their plan? Something jingled, far away. Lily had heard it once already, just before Mr. Plinker had caught her. It was the bell above the workshop door.

Someone else had come into Plinker's Timepieces. It couldn't be a customer, not at this hour.

"Mr. Ozinda!" Lily shouted, running back down the tunnel to the glass window. "Oh, please let it be you!"

Lily gazed out, hoping and hoping, wanting so badly to hear the sing-song rhymes of her Spanish safekeeper.

But the person in the doorway only said three words. And none of them rhymed.

"Release Lily. Now."

"Doctor Gulliver!" Mr. Plinker was astonished. "I heard you leave earlier. I assumed you were gone from my attic for good."

"I have been on a wild-goose chase," answered Gulliver wearily. "Or rather, a wild-parrot chase. Which led me back here."

Without thinking, Lily had drawn Stabber the moment Gulliver had appeared. But the needle wasn't aimed at him. It hovered over her own heart.

Because now that seemed like the only escape.

Mr. Plinker had put the Waste-Not Watch on Finn. He had left Mr. Ozinda in a gutter to die. And now Gulliver was here. What hope did she have?

Gulliver stepped into the workshop. His face was dark and thunderous, and the wind had swept his thin hair into a gray frizz. It was as if a tiny storm cloud had gathered on his head.

And as Lily pointed Stabber at her heart, the storm cloud seemed to break open and pour down Gulliver's cheeks. He began to cry.

"Look at us," he wept. "Look at us yahoos. We kidnap children from their homes. We keep them in cages. We turn them into slaves. We are monstrous. Monstrous."

Lily's grip on Stabber faltered. Gulliver carried on.

"I thought Lily would change us all," he said as his tears pattered on the floor. "And she has. But not for the better. We have become even more selfish and cruel than ever. I should never have taken her from Lilliput. Never. I will burn my book. The world must never know about Gulliver's travels."

Stabber dropped from Lily's hands. Why was Gulliver saying this? How could he have changed so quickly? Lily thought of the moons she had spent desperately trying to convince him to take her back. He had to be lying. He had to. She couldn't believe him.

Then suddenly Lily understood. Gulliver was a man of science. And now that he had left the attic he could see proof. It was right in front of his eyes—the evidence that he was wrong.

"I have made such a terrible mistake." He wiped his eyes. "But I will do what I can to put it right. Give Lily to me. I am going to take her home."

"Wait," said Mr. Plinker softly. "Lily is going to make me a fortune. How can she do that if she leaves with you?"

"If a fortune is what you want, Mr. Plinker, then a fortune I will give you." As Gulliver spoke, he brought a heavy leather sack from his pocket. He loosened the drawstring and poured the contents out slowly onto his hand.

Lily gasped.

Mr. Plinker squinted and leaned forward. "What is that? Dust? Sand?"

But it wasn't either.

"*Sprugs!*" Lily breathed.

In Gulliver's palm were hundreds upon hundreds of gold coins, each one about the size of a pinhead.

"*Sprugs,*" said Gulliver. "Four hundred gold *sprugs*. I was given them many years ago, on an island very close to Lilliput called Blefescu. They are pure gold, but quite useless to me. I tried to use them as proof that the island exists. Parliament dismissed them as forgeries. You can have them all, if you will only let Lily and your apprentice free." Gulliver hung his head in shame. "Do not make the same mistake that I did. Please, Mr. Plinker. Let them go."

Lily and Finn gaped at the pile of money. It was a Lilliputian fortune, but was that enough? Would the miniature coins buy their freedom?

She glanced at Mr. Plinker. A little line of drool fell from his open mouth and he wiped it away. "So you will give me all of these...these *sprugs?*"

"Every single one," Gulliver answered. "I am offering you Lily's weight in gold. What do you say?"

The clock maker stepped closer to the pile of *sprugs* and inspected them. A sly look rustled across his face, and then was gone. "We have a deal," he said. "I am not interested in Lily—just the fortune that she will make me. If I take these *sprugs*, I shall be rich far quicker." The clock maker gave Finn an icy stare. "And you can have my apprentice too. He is worthless to me."

Lily looked on uneasily as Gulliver tipped the gold *sprugs* into Mr. Plinker's hands. The clock maker had a cheerful smile on his face, but it was only a mask—when she looked at his eyes they were cold slits.

It's a trick, she realized. *He's lying. He wants us all. Me, Finn, and the sprugs as well.*

"I have Lily locked in here," said Mr. Plinker, showing Gulliver the Astronomical Budgerigar. "Move away, Finn. Just let Gulliver reach in and pick her up."

Lily frowned. Mr. Plinker wasn't telling Gulliver to reach in through the window—he was telling him to put his hand right in between all the sharp-toothed cogs.

She scooped Stabber from the floor again, her heart racing. Something terrible was about to happen.

"Don't do it!" Lily yelled. "It's a trap!"

But it was too late. Before Gulliver could pull back his hand, Mr. Plinker seized the windup mechanism of the Astronomical Budgerigar and, with a murderous grin, he twisted it clockwise. The clock shuddered into life.

36

Boom & Break

It was like being inside a battle. All around Lily there was utter pandemonium. Cogs clashed together like shields, springs stabbed out like spears, and the Astronomical Budgerigar began tearing itself to pieces.

Gulliver's scream echoed around and around the clock. It was the loudest, most terrible sound Lily had ever heard, and she knew he had not been able to jerk his hand from the clock in time.

She ran down through the tunnel, back toward Swift. She had to get on that saddle. Any second now the clock would strike one, and the perch would whoosh Swift out into the workshop. Or the cogs would drag Lily into their screeching whirligig and it would all be over.

She jumped desperately for the saddle, but Swift reared up again and she slid down his back, plunging toward the grinding cogs.

Her fingers found the tip of a feather, and she jerked to a stop, dangling from Swift's tail. The bird cried out and shook from side to side. Lily's blue slippers fell from her feet, and the clock shredded them in seconds. Her toes wriggled in the air, hovering above the gnashing cogs.

The feather slipped a bit more through Lily's fingers and her feet almost plunged into the machinery. She pulled her knees up to her chest and hung there, suspended. Slipping bit by bit...

"Murderer!" she heard Finn yelling out. "Murderer! Mur—"

Click went the door at the end of the tunnel. Ping went the spring below the perch. And the Astronomical Budgerigar struck one.

Behind the perch a spring released, and Lily and Swift shot through the clock's tunnel like a bullet in the barrel of a gun. Out into the workshop they tumbled, as Swift unfolded his wings.

And flew.

Behind them the Astronomical Budgerigar tore itself to bits. Cogs whizzed through the air like pinwheels, shooting sparks. They sliced candlesticks in half and buried themselves in the walls. One of them passed by Swift's wing in a blur and almost ripped Lily in two.

Finn and Mr. Plinker dived for cover just as the Astronomical Budgerigar collapsed into a pile of springs and spokes.

Up in the air, Lily clung on desperately as Swift corkscrewed around the room, dodging the clockwork missiles. Dizziness overwhelmed her and she lost her grip.

"*Skee, skee!*" she called out as she fell. "Help me, Swift! I'm falling!"

Swift dived down to try and catch her, but he was too late. Lily fell onto a mound of greasy, smelly rope.

"Urgh," she groaned. "What is this?"

With a jolt, she realized it was hair.

Lily had fallen onto Mr. Plinker's head.

She scrambled to her feet just as his hand reached up to grab her. Drawing Stabber again, Lily lashed out with the needle, hearing the clock maker's howl of rage.

Above her, Swift veered away from the clock maker. Lily jumped up again, trying to catch ahold of his tail or his feet, but he flew too fast and she missed.

Then Mr. Plinker tipped back his head and she slid down his forehead, his oily hair slipping through her fingers as she tried to stop her fall. As Lily bounced down his nose, the clock maker tried to snatch her again, but missed and hit himself in the face. Lily skidded over his lips and toppled off his warty chin, into empty air.

Mr. Plinker's hands reached up to trap her, but they came together in a clap, empty. She plummeted, waiting for the sickening *splat* on the floorboards...but it never came.

Because, when Lily opened her eyes, Finn had reached out and caught her.

"You escaped!" he said.

"That's right." She plunged her hand into the Waste-Not Watch. "And now it's your turn."

In a moment, her hands were around Finn's wasted seconds. They flew out of the clock again, until the strap was so loose it slipped from his wrist and the watch tumbled to the floor.

Finn was free.

"No!" snarled Mr. Plinker, seeing he was about to lose both Lily and Finn forever. He aimed a vicious kick at his apprentice, sending Finn hurtling back into the wall. The impact sent Lily flying from his hand. She soared across the room, plowing feet first into the ashes of the unlit fireplace.

Lily dragged herself choking from the cinders, eyes streaming. Finn had crumpled on the floor in a heap, Swift spinning around his head.

Mr. Plinker scooped up the Waste-Not Watch and pinned Finn against the wall.

I have to get Mr. Plinker's attention. I have to draw him away from Finn.

Lily looked up at Swift, still circling around the room and crying out in a panic. He was her only hope.

"Swift!" she called desperately. "Fly down here! Down to the fireplace and then up the chimney! Up the chimney!"

But all that came back to Lily were her own words, echoed and slightly changed.

"Chimney! Chimney!"

Lily stared in confusion up the chimney as her echo spoke to her again, this time in Spanish: *"Hasta la chimenea!"*

"Señor Chitchat!" she cried as the parrot began to babble down the chimney in a series of high-pitched chirps. He was up on the roof, calling down the flue. But what was he squawking about?

And then she understood at last.

Señor Chitchat was translating.

The parrot was talking in Swiftian so that Swift could understand.

Lily looked up. Above her, Swift circled the room one last time. Then he dived into the fireplace, angled in an impossibly steep climb, and shot past her.

Up the chimney.

Gone.

37

Forgiven & Free

Lily cried out. Swift had Gulliver's map in his saddle. The bird she had to fly and the map she needed to follow had both vanished into the night.

"Don't leave!" she cried in despair. "Not without me!"

Up above, Señor Chitchat cried out: *"Don't leave! Skee, skee, skee!"*

Lily felt a glimmer of hope. The parrot was telling Swift to stay. And if he was talking to Swift, maybe Swift was still up there waiting for her.

"Hold on!" she cried, gripping the brick of the fireplace. "I'm coming!"

Then a hand scooped her up into the air. She screamed and whipped out Stabber, but it wasn't Mr. Plinker. Or Finn. They were both still fighting each other on the other side of the workshop .

"Climb, Lily." Gulliver's voice was tiny and weak like a child's. "Climb up. Get free."

He lifted her as high as he could, and let her go.

Lily stepped onto the chimney bricks, looking down at the hand that held her. It was covered in something sticky and dark. The Astronomical Budgerigar had wounded Gulliver terribly. Whole rivers of blood were flowing out of him, from a dozen different wounds. The glooping, iron smell of it made her gag.

"I'll fix you," she managed to say. "Like I fixed Mr. Plinker."

He shook his head violently. "You can't," he said.

Lily opened her mouth to protest, but then she saw it. The sprung perch from the Astronomical Budgerigar. It had broken off from the clock and stabbed Gulliver like a spear. It was jutting into his heart.

"Forgive me," he said, and his voice filled with panic. "Will you forgive me, Lily?"

Lily looked at him open-mouthed, and searched for an answer. But whatever she said, Gulliver wouldn't hear. His spectacles were like empty windows. There were no longer any thoughts behind them at all.

"I forgive you," she said anyway, hoping that some-where, somehow he was listening.

Then, her eyes blurry with tears, she turned to Mr. Plinker and shouted: "Hey, you *zijji-gunching quog!*"

On the other side of the workshop Mr. Plinker whipped around. He was just about to slip the Waste-Not Watch back over Finn's wrist. The hand that held the watch hovered in the air.

"I'm climbing up this chimney," she said. "And when I get to the top I'm going home. To Lilliput. So if you want me, you're going to have to catch me."

And she began to climb.

Mr. Plinker's eyes slid back and forth. From Lily to Finn. Finn to Lily. He couldn't have them both—he would have to choose.

With a roar of frustration, he dropped Finn and the Waste-Not Watch and lunged for Lily. But his hesitation had cost him precious seconds, and she was already scurrying up the brick out of his reach.

"*Lilliputian!*" he bellowed up the flue. His shout rang in Lily's ears. "You haven't escaped! I'm coming for you!"

Writhing and kicking, Mr. Plinker came up the chimney after her.

Arms aching with the effort, Lily pulled herself a little closer to the sky above. Mr. Plinker's roars made the whole chimney shake, and sent soot tumbling down from above. It fell in her mouth, in her eyes, and up her nose, but she couldn't stop. If she stopped, he would snatch her.

She climbed on, half-blind and half-deaf and half-dead with exhaustion. Below her Mr. Plinker gave chase, but in the cramped chimney his size was not an advantage. The giant had to squeeze himself farther and farther up as the flue became narrower and narrower. He wheezed and spat as the soot covered his face.

But he was still gaining.

His shouts were coming closer.

Lily pulled herself up again, for the last time. She leaned against the bricks, wheezing. Her arms were on fire, her legs were like water. She had nothing left. She couldn't climb any farther.

"You can't escape!" Mr. Plinker choked. His face was transformed into a nightmare, streaked with snot and soot. His fingertips were inches away...

All he had to do was reach out and take her.

Lily drew Stabber, lunging at Mr. Plinker's fingers, ready to fight to the end.

"Come on," she gasped. "Snatch me if you can."

The clock maker reached out, but his fingers got no closer. His grin faded. He kicked again, he wriggled and shook, until his eyes bulged in their sockets. He roared, he screamed, he swore and sobbed, but none of it did any good.

He was stuck.

Lily looked up to the square of sky above as something fell down toward her.

A black shape.

It unfolded.

It flew.

"Swift!" she cried. He had listened. Señor Chitchat had made him understand. Swift had come back to save her.

"*Skee, skee...!*" cried Swift, and Lily smiled and let go of the brick. For a moment she hung in the air, just above Mr. Plinker's straining hand. Then Swift performed his impossible turn. With a bump, Lily landed in his saddle and soared away from the clock maker's grasp.

"*Lilliputian!*" he screamed, one last time.

She shot out of the darkness of the chimney. The world fell away as she and Swift rose up and up and up. She rode a black arrow in the crisp air.

Tugging on the harness, she made Swift spin left and roll right. He dived and did a loop-the-loop. It was as if they were writing a message on the sky. Swift and Lily. Lily and Swift. Together.

It was a single word, just one word, and Swift wrote it over and over again as he flew through the air: *freedom.*

Freedom.

Lily was free.

She let the reins drop slightly, and Swift shot down, whipping around the chimney where Señor Chitchat sat preening his feathers.

"*Adiós, amigos!*" he called.

Waving, Lily arrowed past him, down to Tock Lane. Out from the alleyway staggered Mr. Ozinda, covered head to foot in sludge and muck. Lily flew Swift over his head, as Dumpling stared openmouthed and Horatio purred in her arms.

"Farewell, my girl!" shouted Mr. Ozinda. "Adieu to you! Be glad, not sad! Eat well, don't dally, watch for rain! Perhaps we'll see you once again! If not, we'll see you all the same!"

But Lily couldn't leave yet. She wheeled Swift around to stare anxiously at the workshop. She had to know if Finn was safe. But the door stayed shut. No one came out.

"Where's Finn?" she called to Mr. Ozinda as she circled. Swift tugged on the reins, trying to fly south. "Swift wants to leave, he needs to go south! He should have left months ago!"

"Then go!" Finn cried as he burst through the door at last. "Go home, Lily!"

"Good-bye, Finn!" she shouted. "Good-bye! I won't forget! I won't ever forget!"

Swift circled the roof twice, with Lily waving and waving. Finn waved back.

Morning was coming. The sun was a golden cup spilling over the horizon, and the leaves lay crisp and brittle in the trees at the end of the lane, waiting for a cold wind to blow them south.

As her safekeepers watched, Lily turned and flew over London, toward the Thames.

She headed for the horizon.

For home.

For Lilliput.

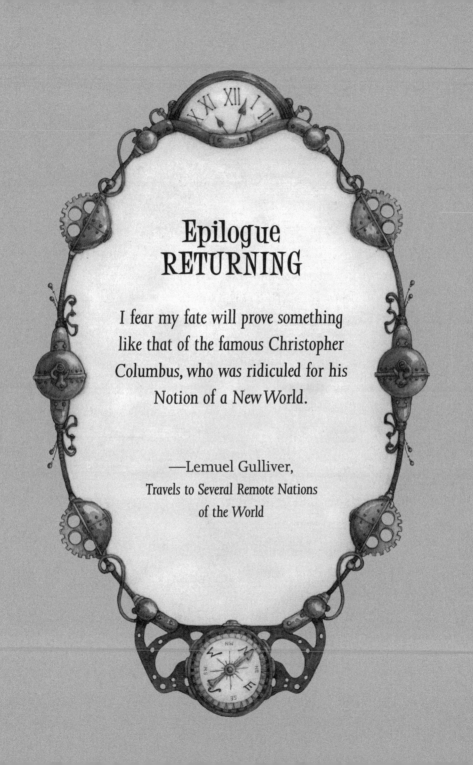

Epilogue
RETURNING

I fear my fate will prove something
like that of the famous Christopher
Columbus, who was ridiculed for his
Notion of a New World.

—Lemuel Gulliver,
*Travels to Several Remote Nations
of the World*

It was spring, and the birds were returning to London. Finn Safekeeping sat on the roof of Plinker's Timepieces, watching them come. With one hand shading the sun from his eyes he scanned the sky. It was very good to sit there on the warm tiles, with his cuffs and collar undone and his skin tingling in the wind.

All around, the world was waking up. Winter was over. Everything was beginning again.

Six months had passed since Lily had left London. Since Gulliver's body had been returned to his family in Nottingham. Since Mr. Plinker had been jailed in the Clink for murder. Since Finn had got himself a new master, who made chocolate instead of clocks.

So much had happened.

So much was about to happen.

Suddenly Mr. Ozinda's voice came up from the street. "Finn? Your adventures are about to begin! Come down quick, or you'll miss them!"

"Coming!" Finn called, still looking at the sky. He couldn't tear himself away. He wanted to stay a little longer. Just a few seconds more.

"If you are coming, you must come right now. The Orinoco sets sail in an hour, my boy!"

Finn sat up with a start and nearly toppled off the roof. "An hour!" he cried, looking down at the Spaniard. "But I haven't packed!"

Mr. Ozinda grinned and held out Finn's sack, crammed full of clothes. "Don't thank me, thank Señor Chitchat. He's the one who remembered."

Finn sank back with relief. "I'm sorry," he blushed. "I'm such a fool. I lost track of time…"

Gripping the chimney, he stood up and looked south, at the Thames running through the city like a vein of silver. The Orinoco was setting off from the docks near Wapping. An hour. He would have to run, and perhaps tail on the back of a carriage, but he would make it. Just.

"Wait any longer, Finn, you may have to swim," Mr. Ozinda yelled up at the roof. "Señora Ozinda does not like to be kept waiting."

Finn knew it. He did not want to disappoint Mrs. Ozinda, especially after she had been so kind and agreed to take him away to sea.

"Come down," said Mr. Ozinda. "You are going to the Americas, where the cocoa beans grow. My lovely Señora Ozinda will show you all she knows—how to spot the finest beans, how to haggle out a sum. So do not sit here, waiting for a bird that might not come."

241

Finn nodded, allowing himself one last look at the birds. There were sparrows squabbling over crumbs in the street. A blackbird singing from a window ledge. A few flustered pigeons listening, too stupid to learn a song.

But no Swift.

"It means nothing, Finn," Mr. Ozinda called. "You know that. Perhaps he has stayed in Lilliput. Perhaps he is roosting somewhere else."

Finn shook his head. "No. A swift comes back to the same nest, the one it leaves behind. He'll be here. He'll roost in Mr. Plinker's chimney. The place where he was born."

Mr. Ozinda shrugged and sighed. "Finn," he said at last. "Even if you do see Swift, it does not prove that Lily made it home. You know that. We did all we could. She knew the risks."

Finn didn't answer. His fingers fiddled with the new silver buttons on the jacket that Mr. Ozinda had bought him. Then his hands dipped into his pocket and took out the Waste-Not Watch.

It was no longer fixed to his wrist. The leather strap had been taken off completely. Instead, it dangled on a chain. The ticking of the jagged iron hand still made him shiver, but Finn had never thought of breaking it. There were times when the Waste-Not Watch still had its uses.

He checked the jagged hand, going tick, tick, tick, telling him what he already knew—this was a waste of time.

It was no use waiting.

Swift wasn't coming back today.

"Will you watch for Swift?" he asked Mr. Ozinda. "Will you let me know if he comes?"

"I will."

"Promise," Finn insisted. "Swear on Dumpling, on Spain, on chocolate itself!"

"I swear," Mr. Ozinda said solemnly.

Finn sighed. He supposed that was good enough. Picking himself up from the tiles, he crawled back through the attic window. With Horatio and Mr. Plinker gone, the mice had moved in. Finn startled one, a little thing with half a tail, nibbling on the bedsheets.

He stood, looking at the birdcage still hanging on a hook above Gulliver's old medicine chest. At the tiny footprints in the spilled candle wax on the desk. Everything was just where it had been all those months ago when he had first crept in through the door. But Lily was gone. The sprugs had all been picked up from the workshop and tossed into the Thames. And Gulliver's Travels wasn't there, either.

At first Finn had wanted to burn the book—to keep Lilliput secret and Lily safe. But eventually he realized that it didn't matter if all of London read it. Without proof, no one would believe a word.

And so they had sent *Gulliver's Travels*, along with his body, up to Nottingham. Mr. Ozinda had said it was only right that Gulliver's family should know what he had died for. Who knew whether they would believe the book.

Whatever happened, *Gulliver's Travels* would forever more be nothing but a story.

Finn ran from the room and down the stairs. He was leaving this damp and ruined workshop, leaving this city, leaving for a great adventure, just like Lily had done.

He burst out of the workshop and onto Tock Lane. Mr. Ozinda threw him the sack, and Finn slung it over his shoulder.

"Now make haste," Mr. Ozinda grinned. "You have no more time to waste! Even your watch thinks so. Look—it has stopped ticking."

Finn looked down at the clock in his hand. It was true. The Waste-Not Watch was completely frozen.

And then up above…

A cry of: "*Skee! Skee!*"

Heart pounding in his chest, Finn whirled around, scanning the sky. A dark shape arrowed through the air and dived down toward the street.

"Look!" Mr. Ozinda gasped. Then he glanced at Finn. "It might not be—"

But Finn was already rushing back up the workshop stairs, dropping his sack on the street. In a moment he was wriggling through the attic window and onto the roof.

"*Skee, skee!*" he heard in the sky above. "*Skee, skee!*"

Finn looked up and saw the bird. The elegant arcs, the sharp turns, the sheer drops, the long, lazy circles...

It had to be Swift. It had to be.

He threw back his head and laughed at the sky. His hand came up to trace the bird's flight in the air. What message was written there, in Swift's sketching on the sky? Had Lily made it? Was she home?

Suddenly Swift swooped down smoothly into his nest. Finn could barely breathe. He ran across the tiles and peered inside the chimney. The bird sat gripping the brick with his stubby little feet, staring at Finn with his head cocked. He had grown bigger and stronger. The silk saddle was still on his back, but there was no rider on him. No Lily.

He was carrying something else.

A small shimmering something, tied to his foot.

Swift flitted from brick to brick and called out again. Slowly Finn stepped closer. He reached a trembling hand to Swift's leg and pulled at the knot of string. The shimmering thing came loose, and Finn snatched it before it fell down the chimney. It was a glass bottle, the size of a raindrop.

He held it in his palm, the way he had once held her. Then he pulled away the speck of cork that stoppered the bottle and shook out a roll of paper as thin as a sheet of skin.

It was a message. A message in a bottle.

Hardly daring to breathe in case he blew it away, Finn teased open the paper. There were no words. Just a picture, the size of a stamp.

She was older, but still the same. Her hair was a wisp of smoke and her eyes shone. Together with Swift she stood on the shore. She had let the bird's reins drop to put her arms around her nana. There were people surrounding them, for as far as Finn could see. Cheering and smiling, laughing and crying. Welcoming Lily home.

Afterword

I was with my brother on the Cornish cliffs. We were chatting, making jokes, but mostly we were just walking and watching the sea and stone crash against each other. The gulls were wheeling in the precipice right next to us, an arm's reach away.

It was a grotty, blustery day and my mum and dad were far behind us—I could make out their brightly colored coats as they made their way along the path. They looked tiny—like jelly babies.

It was one of those moments where everything connected—the bluster of the wind, the scary sea, how small my parents seemed out there, and the birds. Maybe if I'd have been on my own, I would have said nothing. But I had an audience. I turned to my brother and I started to tell him Lily's story.

As soon as I'd finished, two marvelous things happened. First, we all went for a cream tea (yum). Then, I made a decision: I was going to write down Lily's story. I was going to make it into a book.

But I felt bad. Guilty. Lily's story was full of someone else's ideas—his name was Jonathan Swift, and he wrote a book about the tiny island of Lilliput and the people who lived there. His book is called *Gulliver's Travels*.

Could I write a story about a Lilliputian too?

Wasn't that stealing? Or copyright infringement? Or plagiarism?

It wasn't like I could ask Jonathan Swift for his permission, either. He died in 1745. Darn. It looked like I was 267 years too late.

Suddenly, my cream tea didn't taste so creamy.

Thank goodness for Mum, is all I can say.

"Miffs fin rer fubric fromay," she cried out to me, halfway through munching a scone.

No one understood her at all. We wiped the scone crumbs from our eyes and waited for her to chew a bit more.

"*Gulliver's Travels* is in the public domain," Mum said at last. "That means, because it is so old, it belongs to everyone."

I stared at her. She was right. *Gulliver's Travels* belongs to the public. That means me, you, him, her, the Queen's butler...

In short: everyone!

Which meant I could *definitely* give myself permission to write a sequel to a book I hadn't written in the first place.

And so I have.

In fact, as I began to research *Gulliver's Travels*, I discovered that I was being even less original than I had first thought. When it was published in October 1728, *Gulliver's Travels* was about as original as you can get. It was a book of "firsts." It featured:

- The first ever computer, which Swift calls "The Engine"
- The first ever bespectacled hero (take that, Harry Potter!)
- The first ever mention of aerial bombardment

As well as plenty of other cool stuff. Everyone loved it. But people weren't happy with just a first helping. They wanted seconds too. In fact, as soon as *Gulliver's Travels* was published, people began to carry on his story. The book inspired spin-offs, sequels, poems, pamphlets, and films. It still does. *Gulliver's Travels* is also the first story in English literature to inspire what we now call "fan ficton"—a story inspired by someone else's story.

Writers wrote hundreds—literally hundreds—more adventures, all set in Gulliver's world. These stories have a collective name, "Gulliverania."

Hmm, I thought. If all those famous, important, brilliant writers can do it, why can't I?

So I have.

You should too. *Gulliver's Travels* is like a wonderful collection of old keys. Once you've got hold of them, they'll start opening doors in your head that have never been opened before. You'll find places where islands float in the air, horses talk, and scientists try to extract sunbeams from cucumbers. Weird places, wild places, funny places. Places full of stories. Places everyone should visit.

So go on. Follow Gulliver. Get travelling. And if you do visit anywhere interesting, I'd love to hear from you…

twitter: @samgayton
email: samgayton@samgayton.com
web: www.samgayton.com

A list of some of my favorite Gulliverania:

As soon as *Gulliver's Travels* was published, Alexander Pope (who was good friends with Jonathan Swift) wrote a poem called a "Lilliputian Ode," which has two syllables in every line. It's about Gulliver putting out a fire in the Lilliputian palace by weeing on it.

That same year, Murtagh McDermot wrote a sequel where Gulliver begins to travel again, and this time visits the men in the moon. (This was before we knew that the moon is a big dead ball of dust, of course.)

After Swift's death, someone else wrote a story about the adventures of Gulliver's son, who was half-Lilliputian (and so about three feet tall).

In 1946, T. H. White wrote *Mistress Masham's Repose*, which is about a young girl who discovers a group of Lilliputians living in her old English country house.

In 1986 Studio Ghibli released their first ever motion picture, *Laputa: Castle in the Sky*, about a boy's quest to find the mythical floating island of Laputa (which Gulliver visits in his third travel).

—**Sam Gayton**